A Skeleton in the Closet

by

Judith K. Ivie

A Kate Lawrence Mystery from

Mainly Murder Press
PO Box 290586
Wethersfield, CT 06109-0586
www.mainlymurderpress.com

Mainly Murder Press

Senior Editor: Paula Knudson
Copy Editor: Jennafer Sprankle
Cover Designer: Patricia L. Foltz

All rights reserved

Mainly Murder Press
www.mainlymurderpress.com

Copyright © 2009 by Judith K. Ivie
ISBN 978-0-615-26899-6

Published in the United States of America

2009

Mainly Murder Press
PO Box 290586
Wethersfield, CT 06109-0586

Dedicated with Appreciation to:

Shireen and John Aforismo
for generously allowing me to use the
Silas W. Robbins House
as the inspiration for this
work of fiction

and

Elaine, Melissa, and
all of the other good folks at the
Wethersfield Historical Society

Books by
Judith K. Ivie

In the Kate Lawrence Mystery Series:

A Skeleton in the Closet

Murder on Old Main Street

Waiting for Armando

Don't Say Goodbye to Love

Calling It Quits:
Turning Career Setbacks to Success

Working It Out:
The Domestic Double Standard

Preface

Those of you who are already familiar with the Silas W. Robbins House (No, that's not it on the cover.) at 185 Broad Street in Wethersfield, Connecticut, don't need to be told that *A Skeleton in the Closet* is entirely a work of fiction, but others may. Purchased in 2001 by Shireen and John Aforismo, and restored to its current splendor over the ensuing six years, the actual SWR House is a French Second Empire treasure with a fascinating history dating back to 1873. I urge you to discover its real story for yourselves at <u>www.silaswrobbins.com</u>.

As did most of the other residents of Wethersfield, I followed the progress of the restoration with excitement and rejoiced at the grand opening of the Aforismos' bed & breakfast in October 2007. When I approached Shireen and John about a year earlier with the idea of setting one of my Kate Lawrence mysteries in the house, they took a shine to the idea. We then spent a delightful, if somewhat unconventional, afternoon exploring the house from top to bottom to identify likely hiding places for a body. It's not everyone's idea of a good time, but I had a ball.

A Skeleton in the Closet is not the actual story of the Silas W. Robbins House, but it was inspired by the grand old structure and by the Aforismos, who allowed this author to play a game of "What if ...?" I am very grateful and sincerely hope you enjoy the results.

Judith K. Ivie
February 2009

One

The long, wet spring had finally turned the corner into a Connecticut summer so glorious that the residents of Old Wethersfield decided among ourselves that it had probably been worth the wait. Now that we were into June, the houses on both sides of the Broad Street Green boasted lush lawns and flower beds glowing with every color imaginable under canopies of trees in full leaf. The fields behind the farmhouses showed promising signs of the sweet corn to come, and although I knew very well that I had another month to wait, I was already salivating at the thought of wolfing down a tomato so fresh it was still warm from the sun.

The grand old specimens of oak, elm and beech that anchored the green itself dozed in the morning sunshine, no doubt congratulating themselves on having survived yet another New England winter. Property was proudly maintained here, and nearly every Cape Cod, Colonial, Victorian and farmhouse along our route shone with fresh paint and liberally applied elbow grease.

Usually, my daughter Emma and I hiked the loop from the Law Barn on Old Main Street, where our respective businesses were housed, to the Wethersfield Cove and back, but we varied our route occasionally to check out properties for sale in different neighborhoods. It's not everyone's idea of a good time, but we both have reason to be interested in local real estate. Along with my partners, Margo Farnsworth and Charlene Putnam, I own MACK Realty. Emma, a paralegal, and her friend Isabel, who had just passed her bar exam, were launching a real estate law practice in the Law Barn's spacious loft. House sales were booming in what had to be the last of a sustained hot market, and our morning constitutionals gave us an opportunity to mix a little business with pleasure before the workday claimed us.

We slowed our pace as we approached the little pond on the corner of Spring Street, where a dozen geese and a sprinkling of ducks habitually summered. Emma, her older brother Joey, and I shared a fondness for all types of critters, and we liked to follow the progress of the fuzzy ducklings and goslings as they morphed into sleek adulthood, ready for their fall migration to more hospitable winter quarters. For the past few years, a pair of black-legged mute swans had also selected our little pond as their summer home. Since swans are both bossy and territorial, their presence didn't please the rest of the feathered inhabitants, but the human visitors were delighted. This year's hatch had produced four splendid cygnets.

This morning, the elegant twosome seemed to be sleeping late, as they were nowhere in sight. I hadn't visited the pond in several weeks, and I was eager to see the babies and be sure that all were present and accounted for. The few Canadian geese who had not been run off, plus a small number of sturdy mallards, were taking advantage of the swans' absence by preening their feathers on the grass near us.

"Eeuuuww, what's that?" Emma stood on the bank and twisted her long, ash blonde hair into a high ponytail as she scanned the bank on the far side of the pond, squinting in the bright sunlight. She leaned forward and frowned. "It looks like a hairy chicken."

I peered in the direction she was pointing. Though my eyes aren't as young as my daughter's, I could make out what did indeed look something like a chicken covered in dryer lint wriggling in the tall grass. One scrawny, unattractive wing stretched out briefly. Instinctively, Emma shrank away, but the sight made me smile. "Maybe it's a baby buzzard," she ventured. "Do buzzards live around here?" The creature in question now unfolded a long, wobbly neck and lifted its head. Emma looked at me in bewilderment. "What in the world ..."

Before I could speak, her question was answered. Out of the marsh grasses to the left of the mysterious specimen strutted two magnificent swans, herding three more of their babies. When the adults had their four hideous offspring satisfactorily corralled, they all filed into the water. First came Dad, gliding slowly across the still surface. The four youngsters paddled after him furiously. I noticed that one of them was a bit smaller than the others, but he or she seemed to be able to keep up just fine. Mom brought up the rear. "Baby swans!" Emma crowed in disbelief. "Hans Christian Andersen sure had that ugly duckling thing right. I've never seen one before, have you, Mamacita? It's kind of like with pigeons. You know there must be babies, but I don't know anyone who has actually seen one."

3

Emma's nickname for me was a hangover from a long-ago semester of high school Spanish. After ten years, it had almost stopped annoying me. "They're cygnets, technically speaking, and yes, I've seen them before. They're absolutely adorable when they're first hatched, just like ducklings. This is their awkward adolescence, but they'll morph into beauties in a few more weeks." We stared at the gawky youngsters as their proud parents continued their circuit of the pond, oblivious to our opinions. I checked my watch. It was only 7:15, still too early for the dog walkers and the baby strollers.

I scanned the neighboring apartment buildings to be sure we wouldn't be disturbed for a while longer, then eased open the trunk of my Altima and extracted the digital camera I kept handy. I wanted to be able to get a closer look at these fascinating babies when I got back to my computer.

I rejoined Emma at the water's edge next to the sign that read, "Don't Feed the Animals" and hoped once again that it was keeping people from tossing bread, crackers and the other awful stuff they had been taught by their misguided parents to throw into the pond for the geese and ducks who summered there. They meant it kindly, of course, but the truth was that the starchy stuff swelled the birds' bellies, spread avian botulism through the excessive droppings that resulted, and kept the birds from foraging for the seeds, aquatic grasses, and submerged pond weeds that constituted their ideal diet, supplemented with a few invertebrates, fish eggs and small fish.

I took two careful photos of the little family and checked the results in my viewer before turning the camera off. "There. Now I have proof that baby swans are ugly. I wonder when they'll get pretty this year?"

"I hope it's not before I get back." Emma looked a bit wistful as she smoothed her hair out of her hazel eyes, so much like my own. She was a slightly shorter, sturdier version of me at the same age, and her smile lit up any room she entered. Her brother Joey had dipped equally into both sides of his gene pool and wore my face atop his father's frame. On him, I had to admit the combination looked good, and more than a few young women seemed to agree.

"When is that again?" I asked as we headed back toward the Broad Street Green, where our cars were parked.

"Six weeks from Saturday, the end of July."

Today's walk would be our last for several weeks, I reflected. This afternoon Emma would leave for Boston, about one hundred miles northeast of Wethersfield, to study in preparation for the National Federation of Paralegal Associations' advanced competency exam. The designation of Registered Paralegal would enhance her new business's credentials, which was a good idea for a pair of twenty-eight-year-olds striking out on their own.

"How is Officer Ron taking your impending separation?" I twitted her. Ron Chapman of the Wethersfield Police Department was Emma's latest beau.

"Not well, but that's okay. It will be good for him to miss me. He's coming up for the Fourth of July concert by the Charles River. A little absence will make for a hot reunion," she teased back, digging an elbow into my ribs.

"That's way too much information for your mother," I complained. "Knock it off, or I'll force you to listen to the lurid details of my sex life." I did a Groucho Marx eyebrow wiggle.

She feigned shock. "You and Armando *have* a sex life? At your advanced ages? Amazing." Armando Velasquez was my steady man, a handsome South American transplant who could still make my middle-aged heart flutter like a teenager's after eight years together—when we weren't bickering, that is. Unfortunately, at present, we were. The topic was moving in together, which we were days from doing. As devoted as we were to each other, and as much as we loved being together, we were both reluctant to give up the freedom of solo living we had enjoyed since our respective divorces many years ago. Armando seemed to think we would be fine under the same roof. I wasn't as confident.

I sighed as we approached our cars and tried to ignore the anxiety that nibbled at my midsection. "I'll come by and take baby swan pictures once a week or so. I can e-mail them to you so you can keep up with the little uglies' progress."

"Great! You can send them right to my cell phone." Emma owned every electronic gadget on the market, which I realized was age appropriate, but it astounded me that she operated all of them with ease. I could barely manage to place a call on my cell phone, and I seriously doubted my ability to send digital photos to hers, but I decided to let her keep her illusions about her mother's technical ability for a while longer.

"I'm going home to pack. I'll call you later to say goodbye." Emma was quite aware of my angst and opted not to drag out our farewell. She hugged my neck, climbed into her Saturn, and zoomed off, leaving me gazing after her with mixed feelings. Officer Ron might be okay with Emma's newfound independence, but I wasn't sure I was.

Emma and her brother Joey, seventeen months older than she, had both preferred to stay close to home until recently, content to live within a tight circle of friends and family. About two years ago, Joey had suddenly become restless, acquired a commercial driver's license, and now led the gypsy existence of a long distance trucker.

To everyone's amazement, he loved it. Six nights a week, he lived in his surprisingly comfortable tractor, which, when hooked up to a trailer, formed the seventy-three-foot rig in which he moved back and forth across the country. The space behind the driver's seat resembled a very small apartment and contained bunk beds, a small refrigerator, cupboards and shelves, a television/DVD player, laptop computer, and a satellite radio dish. The truck stops he frequented offered shower rooms and power hook-ups and even air conditioning or heat, depending upon the season, which was provided through a window vent.

One night a week, he turned up from Denver or San Diego or Atlanta to spend the night at my Wethersfield condominium, wolf down a home-cooked meal, and play with Simon and Jasmine, my aged housecats. The rest of the time, he was seeing more of the United States, Canada, and even Mexico than I ever would, and I had a wall map full of push-pins to prove it.

Now Emma was heading for the big city, and I wasn't sure how I felt about it. I was proud of her, certainly, but there was something more. Fear? No. I chuckled as I unlaced my Avias and stuck my feet into the sandals I wore to work these warm summer days. Emma was nobody's fool. Her father and I had raised her to take care of herself. She would be gone for only a few weeks. More likely, I was a little envious. My own school days in Boston, a city I continue to love, had ended more than thirty years ago, but the spirit of the perpetual teenager that still inhabited my middle-aged body remembered the sounds and scents of summer evenings by the Charles River, enjoying the Boston Pops concerts with beaux of my own. It had been pretty heady stuff then. For Emma's sake, I hoped it still was.

* * *

"Eeeuuwww, what's that?" This time the comment came from Jenny, the pretty youngster who worked as our receptionist, as I entered the Law Barn's lobby through the back door. Frowning, she scanned the newspaper clipping she held in one hand, then turned it sideways to examine something written in the margin. An envelope dangled from her other hand. She wrinkled her nose in disgust, but on her, it was merely cute. No one looking at Jenny for the first time would guess that the petite brunette was a second-year law student at the University of Connecticut, working days to earn the tuition for her night classes, in which she ranked solidly among the top ten percent. "Listen to this, Kate." She read aloud:

June 14 / 3:05 p.m. US/Eastern, STORRS, Conn. (AP) Within the next few weeks, New Englanders will have the opportunity to see and smell one of the strangest productions of the vegetable kingdom: the titan arum, which features a gigantic bloom — and a mighty stench akin to that of decaying flesh — is expected to open sometime near the end of June at the University of Connecticut's Department of Ecology and Evolutionary Biology Conservatory.

Currently, the flower bud is more than three feet high and growing by several inches each day. The plant growth facilities manager estimates the plant will flower between June 28 and July 2. Mature flowers are about 6 feet high and 3 feet across, shaped like an urn, with a tall spike rising from the center. The colors of the corpse flower — a sickly yellow and blackish purple — imitate a pot roast that sat out in the sun for a week. The fragrance is universally described as being powerful and revolting, with elements of old socks, dead bodies and rotten vegetables. As if that isn't weird enough, the corpse flower is actually warm-blooded, heating itself up at the height of flowering, probably to help spread its putrid odor and attract the flies that will pollinate the plant.

I leaned over Jenny's shoulder to have a look at the accompanying photo of the botanical phenomenon, which resembled a tightly closed, three-foot-tall lily bud. "Now there's something only a botanist could love." I yielded my spot to Margo, who had joined us on her way to refill her coffee mug. Incredibly, she had risked wearing white linen to the office, but I had to admit that the fitted sheath complemented her fair coloring and blonde chignon exquisitely. Rhett Butler, the chocolate Labrador Retriever who was Margo's constant companion, nuzzled my ankle, and I obliged with a head scritch while his mistress gazed, awestruck, at the corpse flower bud.

"Oh, my," Margo gasped. "That is the most phallic flower I have ever seen, Sugar. Why, it's absolutely disgustin'!" She winked at me behind Jenny's back.

"Since when do you use the words 'phallic' and 'disgusting' in the same comment?" I countered. Southern belle though she was, Margo's avid interest in men made her resemble Samantha Jones more closely than Scarlett O'Hara. Since last fall, she had been focusing on Lieutenant John Harkness, who headed the Wethersfield Police Department's detective division. He was also Ron Chapman's boss. To everyone's amazement, John had abandoned his dour professional persona and was thriving under the attentions of my libidinous partner. "Who sent us the clipping, and what's that scribbling down there on the corner?"

Jenny handed me the clipping, which was actually a computer print-out of an article from an internet news website, and took a closer look at the envelope. "There's no return address, but it's postmarked Storrs," she noted. Do you have a friend at UConn, Kate?"

The University of Connecticut was located in Storrs. "Not that I'm aware of. Why? Was it addressed to me?"

Jenny inspected the address again. It had been block printed in blue felt pen. "Mmmm, no, it wasn't. It just says Mack Realty in upper and lower case, as if the person who sent it doesn't know that M-A-C-K is an acronym of the first letters of Margo, Charlene and Kate." She handed the envelope to Margo and looked at us expectantly. "What do you think?"

I held the print-out closer to the lamp on Jenny's desk. The Law Barn's loft had windows and skylights, but downstairs, only the offices at the rear of the first floor enjoyed natural light. The lobby, which occupied the center of that level, was always a bit dim, so we kept a variety of table lamps on during the day to brighten things up. I turned the sheet of paper sideways and peered at the scribbles in the margin, apparently made with the same blue felt pen that was used on the envelope. "It is reported commonly that there is fornication among you," I read with difficulty and looked up. "A Bible verse maybe?" I had been raised as a Lutheran, but my adult attitude toward organized religion was distinctly agnostic, and my remembrance of Bible verses was sketchy.

Margo took a look. "Sure sounds like one to me, Sugar, if I'm rememberin' all those Sunday mornins' I spent yawnin' at the First Baptist Church of Atlanta correctly. And what's this last part? 'And it shall come to pass that instead of sweat ... no, make that sweet ... smell there shall be stink.' Is that a reference to the absolutely revoltin' plant in this news article?"

"I guess," I responded doubtfully, "but what does one thing have to do with the other? And why does someone want to bring fornication and large, smelly plants to our attention?" We looked blankly at each other, then back to Jenny.

"My guess would be some religious zealot has it in for one of you," she announced. "He or she probably doesn't like the fact that all of us unmarried females are breaking at least one of the Commandments on a regular basis." She smiled sunnily. "You know, Kate and Armando ... Margo and John ... Emma and Ron ... oops! Sorry, Kate. I keep forgetting that you're Emma's mom."

My smile was thin. "I believe you said 'all of us,' which would include you, would it not?" I said tartly. Margo giggled, and Jenny started to squirm. The telephone rang, and she snatched it off the hook gratefully.

Momentarily stumped, we left the article and its envelope on Jenny's desk and headed for the coffeemaker. Along with the photocopier, it stood in a little alcove to the left of the lobby. Rhett Butler kept us company, no doubt hoping for a handout from the jar of dog treats that sat next to the coffeemaker. "So what's on everybody's agendas today?" I inquired as I slid a pre-measured filter pack into the plastic basket and poured water into the top of the machine. Making coffee for the junior associates had been one of Margo's duties at the Hartford law firm where she, Charlene and I had worked before we joined forces to open the realty office, and she flatly refused to do it again outside of her own kitchen. I didn't blame her.

"I've got showings scheduled from nine-thirty on at Vista Views," she began, referring to the new active adult community for which we served as rental agents. "Then a quick manicure at one o'clock." She tsk-ed over the state of her fingertips. They looked fine to me, but when it came to the fine points of personal grooming, Margo's standards were higher than mine. "After that, it's paperwork and more paperwork unless ..." hope brightened her expertly made-up face, "Strutter comes in with a new listin', as I frankly expect she will." Strutter was the nickname of our third partner, Charlene Putnam. Recently remarried and the mother of a young son from her first, long-ago marriage, Strutter was a drop-dead gorgeous native of Jamaica. Soft curls fell to her shoulders, and eyes the color of the Caribbean sparkled in her beautiful, brown face, which topped a figure to die for and legs up to here. No one who had ever seen Charlene strut her stuff ever questioned the sobriquet.

"Where is Strutter anyway?" I questioned, filling Margo's mug and then my own. I pointed at the dog treats and raised an eyebrow. Margo shook her head, and we carried our coffee down three steps to the MACK Realty office off the lobby at the rear of the Law Barn. I sat at the desk, and Margo arranged herself on the comfortable sofa and fired up her laptop. Rhett flopped at her feet, sighed once, and fell instantly asleep. He wasn't as young as he once was, and he needed his naps so that he could keep a properly watchful eye on the back yard when Margo took him out to his spacious pen.

"I saw her checkin' the phone messages earlier," she said now, squinting a little as she scrolled through her emails. She resisted wearing her stylish computer glasses, even though I had pointed out the little frown line forming between her exquisitely groomed eyebrows. "There was one from Ada Henstock—you know, one of those darlin' little ol' gals who live over on the Broad Street Green. She wanted our advice on somethin' to do with that enormous house she and her sister own near the Anderson Farm … the French Second Empire with the mansard roof."

Known locally as The Henstock Girls at the age of eighty plus, the Misses Ada and Lavinia Henstock were fixtures in Old Wethersfield. The story went that although both sisters had been quite appealing in their youth, they were spinsters by choice. They had spurned the advances of many a prospective suitor upon the advice of their dear papa, who had never felt that any of the local gents were quite good enough for his little girls.

The Honorable Reuben Henstock, Esq., widowed shortly after his second daughter was born, had been a tartar of a man who had first served in the Connecticut State Legislature, then been appointed to the bench. He had never remarried, leaving the day-to-day care of his children to a succession of housekeepers, and had presided over trials right up until the day of his death in the late 1960s, when he had gaveled the day's court business to a close and collapsed untidily across his bench.

Since then, the sisters, who were known for their ability to stretch a dollar, had shared their home with a scrawny cat or two, but men seeking their company had been unilaterally turned away.

"Huh!" Emma and I just walked right by that house. What kind of advice?"

"Frankly, we couldn't make much sense of Ada's message. You know how reserved she is, how reserved they both are, when they aren't finishin' each other's sentences, but Ada was practically pleadin' for one of us to come by and let her know how somethin' or other might affect the value of their property. She seemed real upset, and you know how tenderhearted Strutter is. She picked up her purse and ran right on over there to put Miss Ada's mind at ease."

I couldn't help smiling as I imagined Strutter walking her distinctive walk up to the front door of the Henstock house and lifting the big brass knocker. The ladies would be peeking from behind the lace curtains at one or the other of the big front windows. They knew Margo and me by sight, since we had sold a house in that neighborhood while Strutter and John were on their honeymoon, but what they would make of Strutter was anybody's guess. It was safe to say that the elderly sisters' experience of black women had been limited to peremptory exchanges with their dear papa's kitchen help when they were growing up. What they would make of a stylishly clad black businesswoman rapping on their front door, I could not think.

"Well, this has been some Thursday morning so far. I saw the baby swans about an hour ago. They look rather like vultures at this stage, did you know that? Emma is taking off this afternoon for six weeks in Boston, and I'm not at all sure how I feel about that. Some religious fanatic seems to have taken exception to the way we conduct our personal lives, and the Henstock girls are having the vapors. Anything else?" I grinned at Margo as I picked up my phone.

I had learned over the past year that once the phone started ringing, it rarely stopped, and by nine o'clock, the day was officially launched. One call followed another, and I did my best to field inquiries about listed properties, refer buyers to the back-up law firm that was covering while Emma and Isabel got ready to open their doors, and soothe jittery sellers who were anxious to move their properties. A major advantage of having a real estate brokerage in Old Wethersfield is that all of the property that can be developed under current zoning ordinances has pretty much been developed. It's an extremely desirable community, located west of the Connecticut River and south of Hartford, and almost any residential property that comes on the market generates a flurry of interest. Even a house with an in-ground swimming pool and no garage will sell in this community, despite our short summers and long winters. I know, because we've done it. As we tell people over and over again, it's just a matter of matching the right buyer with the right property, and if it takes a little time, well, the deal will be that much sweeter when it's done.

As Margo was preparing to leave for her first appointment, we heard the front doors of the Law Barn crash open. Strutter rushed through the lobby and skittered down the half-staircase to the office, almost falling in her haste. She burst through the doorway looking about as pale as it's possible for a black woman to look. "The Henstock sisters have a skeleton in their closet," she announced.

"Don't they always?" murmured Margo, still focused on her computer screen, "and it's the primmest old gals that usually have the wickedest secrets." She giggled delightedly. "I can hardly wait. Let's hear it." She punched Save, crossed one elegant leg over the other, and gave MACK Realty's third partner her full attention. I stopped making notes to myself at my desk and did the same.

"No, really," insisted Strutter. She collapsed onto the sofa next to Margo and looked from one to the other of us wildly. "Kate, Margo, listen to me. There's a skeleton behind a false wall in an old closet in the Henstock sisters' basement. Literally. It had clothes on, or at least, it used to." She clutched her briefcase to her chest and swallowed hard. "I think I'm going to be sick."

Instinctively, Margo leaned away and pulled her Jimmy Choos out of harm's way. I leaped up, wastebasket at the ready, but Strutter waved me away.

"No, no, I'm not really going to hurl. I just feel queasy, and so would you, if you'd seen what I just saw." She flopped back on the sofa and stuck her legs out in front of her. "I need coffee. No," she amended hastily, holding one hand to her stomach, "make that water. Please," she added feebly, eyes closed.

"You bet, Sugar." Margo practically leaped to her feet, causing Rhett Butler to snap to attention. She hurried out to the water cooler and returned in seconds with a filled paper cup. Strutter sat up and sipped carefully, holding the cup between hands that trembled.

I could stand it no longer. "Charlene Putnam, I love you like a sister, but I'm going to walk over there and shake you if you don't tell us what you are talking about right now."

"Don't make me turn Rhett Butler on you," Margo threatened for good measure. The dog panted happily at the mention of his name. He might lick Strutter to death, I knew, but that was about the extent of her peril.

With an effort, Strutter pulled herself together. "As soon as I parked in front of that big, spooky house, I knew it was a mistake to go inside. There were those crazy old ladies peeking out at me from behind the front curtains, plain as day. Did they imagine I was there to rob them at nine o'clock on a Friday morning? You'd think they'd never seen a black woman on their front porch before." She stopped shaking and took another noisy sip of water, irked by the memory. Margo and I exchanged glances.

"They were raised in another era," I soothed, "and they don't get out much these days either. They probably aren't used to women being business owners, never mind black women."

"Huh! Probably don't know we can vote and own property now and everything," Strutter fumed. Margo snorted, an unattractive habit of hers when something tickled her. "Anyway, I announced who I was, and Miss Ada let me in. At least, I think it was Ada. The bigger one with the kinky permanent wave and the sensible shoes." I nodded. "The wispy one, Lavinia, just kind of fluttered around, waving a hankie and moaning to herself. We went into the front room, the one they'd been using to check me out, and sat on the sofa, and I asked as delicately as I could what had them in such a swivet. I didn't want to be too pushy, them still being in shock at having a sister sitting right there on their sofa and all." Another snort from Margo.

"And what did Ada say?" I prodded in an effort to move this along. Margo checked her watch none too discreetly.

Finally, Strutter kicked it into high gear. "She said they'd about run through all the money from their papa's trust fund, and they were considering selling the house, but some pipes running to the old boiler needed serious repairs, and they'd had a fellow banging around in the basement tearing out walls and bricks, and he found something even worse than the leak, and they needed to know how it might affect the value of the property." She sucked in a breath. We waited.

"It was a skeleton! He found it right there in a closet that had been built next to where the pipes come down next to the furnace. He had to break through the back wall, which was apparently false, because there was another one behind it. He completely freaked, said he didn't want to be involved in any investigation or questioned by the police, and he packed up his tools and ran out of there. For some reason, Ada called us. Naturally, I thought she was hallucinating or seeing shadows, so I had her get me a big ol' flashlight and dragged her down there to show her it had just been some moth-eaten clothes on a hanger or something, and, well," she gulped, "there was a skeleton, or sort of a skeleton. It was more like a dried-up old mummy with scraps of cloth clinging to parts of it." She shuddered.

Margo looked at me and back at Strutter. "But why on earth did Ada call us instead of the police? Did she want to know if they should include the thing in their askin' price?" Strutter was not amused.

"Where are Ada and Lavinia now?" I inserted hastily.

"They're right where I left them in their front parlor, drinking cups of strong, hot tea with lots of sugar. I told them I'd come back here and consult with my partners. I didn't know what else to do, and I surely wanted to get out of there."

I sat on the couch next to her and patted her arm. "Well, of course you did. The question is, what do we do now?"

Margo promptly took charge. "I'm going to call John and ask him to meet you—unofficially, of course—over at the Henstocks," she said, punching numbers into her cell phone, "and then I'm going over to Vista Views for my first showing. I'm already late. Don't worry," she comforted Strutter, who looked stricken at the thought of returning to the Henstock house. "John will take very good care of you. He's the head of the detective division, remember, and very reliable. I have reason to know that he's also the soul of discretion." She winked broadly, trying to get Strutter to smile, but she wouldn't.

"Getting tangled up with you, he'd have to be," was her only comment.

Two

A dark blue Ford sedan was just pulling into the Henstocks' driveway as I crossed from Old Main Street to the Broad Street Green on Garden Street. The car was so remarkable in its unremarkableness that it practically screamed "cop." I parked behind it, and Strutter and I joined Lieutenant John Harkness on the front walk. "John, thanks for coming." For the hundredth time, I noticed how beautifully turned out the lieutenant was, his barbered good looks set off by an immaculate navy blue blazer and pinstriped shirt. A gray silk tie was knotted neatly under his collar, and his cordovan loafers shone with polish. Fair, blue-eyed men sometimes didn't age well, but John Harkness was clearly going to be the exception to the rule.

"Morning, Kate, Mrs. Putnam." No matter how often Margo urged him to do so, John refused to use Strutter's nickname. I had heard him call her Charlene once or twice on a social occasion, but that was as far as his natural reserve would allow him to go. Since this was an official visit, I didn't tease him. "Why don't you bring me up to speed."

Strutter completed a more coherent version of her previous breathless recap just as we reached the front porch of 185 Broad Street. The exotic balustrades and slender columns rising three stories were in a state of genteel dishabille, as was the rest of the imposing structure. Although it had doubtless been grand back in the day, the place now had *money pit* written all over it. *I hope the Henstock sisters aren't about to ask MACK Realty to list it for sale*, I thought distractedly, then pulled my mind back to the problem at hand.

John scribbled a few notes in a leather-bound pocket notebook, nodded once, then bestowed one of his rare smiles on Strutter. "Nothing to worry about, I'm sure. This house dates back to, what, the late 1800s?" He looked to me for confirmation, and I nodded. "You'd be surprised how often a skeleton, or even a partial skeleton, falls out of the walls of these old places or gets dug up in the basement when the owners do major renovations or repairs." Not finding a doorbell, he lifted the ornate knocker on the front door and let it drop.

"Can't say that makes me much happier," Strutter grumbled, but she tucked her handbag firmly under her arm and braced herself to revisit the scene.

The door creaked open two inches, and Ada Henstock peered out at us. John displayed his badge and introduced himself. At first, Ada looked uncertain, but when she spotted us behind him, she threw the door open widely and all but dragged John across the threshhold and into the front parlor. Strutter and I followed. Lavinia Henstock slumped in the corner of a rather musty settee, a damp cloth pressed to her forehead. She opened her eyes and smiled weakly.

"Lavinia, dear, do pull yourself together," Ada urged. "This is Lieutenant John Harkness of the Wethersfield Police Department and Kate Lawrence of MACK Realty. She's Mrs. Putnam's partner along with, oh, what is that flirty southern woman's name?" She frowned at her own forgetfulness. I sneaked a peek at John, whose mouth twitched in amusement.

"Margo Farnsworth," I supplied quickly. "Why don't we all sit down, and you can tell Lieutenant Harkness just what happened."

"Of course, of course." She waved at an assortment of overstuffed furniture that had seen better days, and we all perched uncomfortably on the edges of various pieces. Ada recounted essentially the same story that we had heard from Strutter. Lavinia recovered enough to sit up and embellish her sister's narration with a detail from time to time. "And there it was, a skeleton, right there in that old closet in our basement," Ada finished almost triumphantly. "I saw it with my own eyes, and so did Mrs. Putnam!"

"From what you told me, Dear, it was more of a mummy, really," Lavinia offered diffidently, ineffectually tucking wisps of gray hair behind her ears, "but of course, I didn't actually see it like Ada did." She deferred to her older sister's judgment on the matter. It occurred to me that she had probably been deferring to Ada for most of her life.

John nodded solemnly, then stood. "Thank you. I'm sure this will all be very helpful. And now, I believe I'll just have a look for myself. No, there's no need for you to upset yourselves," he reassured the ladies. "In fact, it would be better if we disturbed the scene as little as possible until I can get a crew in here to investigate things properly." At the mention of an investigation, Lavinia fell back against the cushions and pressed her handkerchief to her eyes once again. "I'll just ask Kate and Mrs. Putnam to come with me as witnesses for the record." He beckoned to us to join him, but Strutter demurred.

"I've seen it once. I don't need to see it again," she begged, and after gazing at her thoughtfully for a second or two, John wisely let her off the hook.

"I'm sure your statement will be sufficient. If you'll stop by the Department sometime today, we'll get that taken care of."

"I'll do that. Now you go right down the hall there past the stairs leading to the second floor. You'll see the door to the basement on the left just before you get to the kitchen." Strutter waved us into the hall and sank back onto a tufted ottoman. She still looked queasy to me, and who could blame her?

I was surprised to find myself a bit jittery as I joined John in the hall. It wasn't as if I had never seen a dead body before. In fact, it was safe to say that over the past couple of years, I had seen more than my share, what with one unexpected development or another. The first had been a murder at the law firm where Strutter, Margo and I had all worked. The second murder had been right here in Old Wethersfield not a year ago. And now here I was again with a Wethersfield police officer at the scene of a grisly death. So much for the peaceful life of small-town New England.

Just as Strutter had said, we passed a wide staircase leading upstairs, then spotted the door to the basement. It was ajar. John paused long enough to snap a thin latex glove on his right hand, then used two fingers to pull the door open. He flipped an ancient-looking switch on the wall inside, and the stairs were weakly illuminated by a bulb hanging from a cord. "How very *Psycho*," I murmured, peering past John. "Do you suppose we'll find the mummified Mrs. Bates rocking in her chair?"

He grinned and led the way into the gloom. We descended the stairs with care, made cautious by thoughts of what we were about to see, as well as by the questionable condition of the steps beneath our feet. At the bottom, the smell of long-established dampness wrinkled my nose and, I admit it, raised a few hairs on the back of my neck. John fished a flashlight out of his pocket and clicked it on. It produced a surprisingly powerful beam, which he panned back and forth slowly across the floor and wall to the right of the stairs. I was glad for the comfort of the light, not to mention the solid police officer standing between me and whatever lurked in the corners.

A pile of old bricks, mortar, splintered wood and other debris attested to the recent demolition of a narrow section of wall at the back of a closet next to a huge, ancient furnace. The new opening revealed a narrow space. John's flashlight shone on the pipes leading to the ancient boiler, one of which was leaking visibly. On the floor at the rear of the closet next to the pipes lay something that looked like a rag along with more bits of mortar and brick. I thought the cloth was dark blue, but I couldn't be certain. Except for some shelving filled with books and files along the back wall of the closet-like space, it was empty. I blinked and looked again. No body, no bones, nothing.

"Well, do you see it?" Strutter, unable to sit still, had followed us to the top of the stairs. "How long do you think that nasty thing has been behind that wall?" The Henstock ladies craned their necks behind her.

"Hard to say," said John, stalling for time and flashing his beam around the remaining walls to augment the meager light from the overhead bulb. The floor seemed to be poured concrete. Both it and the stone walls appeared unbreached and blank. John and I exchanged shrugs and retraced our steps. We peered up at the little group huddled at the top of the stairs. "How long ago did you say you discovered the, uh, remains?"

"It couldn't have been much more than two hours ago," Strutter replied, looking to Ada for confirmation. "Wouldn't you say so?"

Ada nodded vigorously. "Oh, no, it couldn't have been longer than that. The plumber started yelling and clanking around down there, and I went to see what in blazes the trouble was." She swayed a little, and Strutter grabbed hold of her arm. "And then he went tearing up the stairs and out of here, and I climbed back up to tell Lavinia, and then, well, we called you. Isn't that right, Sister?"

"Yes, yes, that's right," Lavinia affirmed. "And then Mrs. Putnam came right over and saw it for herself. She told us to sit tight while she ran back to your offices, and we made ourselves a nice cup of tea ..."

" ... and here you all are," Ada finished up. "We didn't even have time to drink it," she added a bit reproachfully, I felt.

"Well, you may want to make yourselves another cup," said John as we climbed carefully to the top of the stairs and rejoined the trio, "because I'm afraid that what I have to say will surprise you."

"Oh, no! Not more than finding a corpse in the basement," Lavinia gasped, hanging onto her sister for support.

"I believe I would classify it more as a skeleton, Dear, than a corpse. Not so gruesome as a really fresh body, I should imagine."

Unfortunately, I didn't have to imagine, but I was impressed by Ada's zeal for accuracy. Again, John suppressed a smile. "Corpse or skeleton or mummy, it doesn't really matter. The thing is, Ladies, none of those things is in your basement. At least not now," he added hastily as he took note of the shocked and mutinous expressions confronting him. He switched off the light and shepherded us into the kitchen off the hall.

Ada promptly filled the kettle and set it to boil on the front burner of a gas stove, *circa* 1950. I was willing to bet I wouldn't find a microwave oven in this kitchen, and a quick glance around confirmed it. We all took seats at the vast, scrubbed oak table that occupied fully half of the room. I shivered and found myself looking forward to the tea that Lavinia measured carefully into an old-fashioned tea ball as John reported on our findings, or lack thereof, in the basement.

Ada came to sit by Strutter, bound by their common knowledge of what they had seen. "That simply cannot be, Lieutenant Harkness," she asserted firmly. "I know what I saw, and Mrs. Putnam knows what she saw. Why else did that plumber take to his heels, I'd like to know?"

"That's right," Strutter backed her up. "Miss Henstock saw a body in the basement, and I saw it, too. And what about that plumber? Why don't you ask him what sent *him* running out of this house?"

John hastened to ease their rising agitation. "I plan to do just that. I'll just need his name and a phone number, if you have it handy. Thank you," he added as Ada placed a steaming cup of tea before him before serving the rest of us, and Lavinia pushed a bone china creamer and sugar bowl a bit nearer. I imagined the sisters serving the Judge the same way in this very room some forty years ago. It probably gave them comfort to be pouring tea for a man at this table once again.

"Now where did I put that young man's card," Ada asked herself, fumbling through a stack of junk mail and bills on the counter. "I know I have it here somewhere. He gave it to me a few days ago when he was in the neighborhood drumming up business. Ah, here it is." Triumphantly, she presented a white business card to John, which he read aloud.

"Handy Plumber of Connecticut. Licensed, bonded and insured. Eight six oh, six nine oh, fifteen fifteen." He looked questioningly at Ada. "No name, no address. Did he give you a name, Miss Henstock?"

Ada looked flustered. "Why I was almost sure he did ... but now that I think of it, he just knocked on the door here by the kitchen," she waved at the side entrance that was reserved for family members and service people, "and said something like, 'Handy Plumber. You called for service.' And of course I had, so I let him in. He was wearing one of those tool belts filled with things that jangle, and he carried a toolbox. Well, at least there's a telephone number. I spoke to him myself on it, or at least I left a message on his answering machine. You can find him that way, surely?"

John looked again at the card and slowly shook his head. "Doubtful. That's a cell phone number. A cellular phone is portable, you see, not tied to one address. May I use your phone?" Ada nodded at an ancient wall phone by the stove, and John made use of it, checking the number on the card as he pressed the keys. He listened for a few moments and hung up. "No answer. Just a canned message saying that the user is unavailable." Ada and Strutter exchanged crestfallen glances.

"But there must be a billing address for the phone, " Strutter offered.

" … and a name on the account," I chimed in.

"… all of which are traceable, I believe is the expression," Lavinia contributed surprisingly.

John smiled kindly at us all, then finished his tea in a gulp and pocketed the business card along with his notebook. "We're certainly going to try to trace it. In the meantime, I'm going to take a look around outside before I head back to the station. I'll send a forensics team over later to take a closer look at the basement to see what they can turn up. I'd appreciate it if you would keep the door to the basement shut and have everyone stay clear of the area until the team gets here."

"Well, that's certainly fine with me," Ada assured him. "I've had quite enough of that basement and vanishing bodies for the time being."

Lavinia smiled tremulously at John and patted at her rebellious hair once more. "I do hope we haven't been any trouble, Lieutenant. You must be a very busy man."

"That's what the police are here for," he reassured her. *Another conquest,* I thought, amused.

John led the way through the short hallway to the side entrance. "Is this door kept locked?"

The sisters looked at each other for a moment. "Why, no, not during the day," Ada said slowly. "We generally go out this way for the newspaper and the mail and so forth. Of course, we lock up before retiring for the night."

John thanked her for the information and let himself out, but before Strutter and I could follow, Ada put a trembling hand on my arm. Obviously, she was more shaken than she had let on, and my heart went out to her. The morning could not have been an easy one, and even though she was only a year older than her sister, she clearly felt obliged to put on a stoic front for Lavinia, who hovered at her elbow.

"We are so very grateful to you for coming ... grateful to you both," she stressed, including Strutter in her thanks. "If Mrs. Putnam hadn't come so promptly and seen that awful body in the basement ..."

"... why, that nice lieutenant would think we were both as crazy as bedbugs," Lavinia completed the thought. I didn't say so, but I thought they might just be right. Two old ladies living by themselves in that cavernous old house might well be susceptible to an imaginative turn or two.

"I hope I'm not being too inquisitive, but I would have thought that a smaller house would be a lot easier for the two of you to keep up. Why do you prefer to go on living here?" I couldn't help asking.

"Yes, why not move into one of those snug little places they're building over near Jordan Lane, or a great apartment-style condominium like the ones on Ridge Road?" Strutter was obviously as curious as I.

This time, Lavinia answered first. "This is our home. Always has been. I can't imagine living anywhere else. Can you, Dear?" She looked confidently at her sister.

"It's true that I believed that Papa's trust fund would allow us to live out our lives here," Ada hedged uncharacteristically, "but I had no idea how expenses would rise and rise. That hideous war in the Middle East, and the cost of home heating oil. Our taxes ..." She glanced at Lavinia, then quickly averted her eyes. "Well, I guess I don't have to tell you." She cleared her throat. "But we have to face the fact that there simply isn't enough money to keep this place going, and there are major repairs that cannot be ignored any longer. This leak in the boiler pipes is just the tip of the iceberg."

Lavinia's eyes clouded over, and her expression turned sulky. "Ada! You can't mean that you're thinking of selling our home!"

Ada threw us an apologetic glance at Strutter and me for having involved us in this personal conversation, but she held her ground. "Now, Lavinia, you know we've had this conversation before. We're not as young as we once were, and we need to consider the future. Selling this house is our only reasonable alternative, if anyone will have it, that is." She patted her sister's shoulder and shooed her off toward the kitchen. "Why don't you get started clearing away the tea things, and I'll come help in just a moment."

Strutter and I watched Lavinia trudge off, stricken. "We'll do everything we can to help, Ms. Henstock," Strutter offered rashly.

Ada beamed at her. "It's Ada, please, and I felt certain you would."

"Please call me Charlene or Strutter, as my friends do. I answer to either," Strutter smiled back.

I sighed. Selling this monstrosity would be difficult enough. Selling a monstrosity that had recently had a body walled up in the basement might well be impossible.

* * *

"What do you mean, impossible?" Margo and I sat on the back stoop of the Law Barn in the long twilight, alternating swigs from a shared can of Diet Coke. We had already locked up but were sharing a few minutes before heading out. "This is gettin' really interestin'." Mindful of her white linen and her dinner date with John, Margo had centered her svelte haunches on a magazine from our reception area. I wasn't worried enough about my washable Citiknits to bother. "That old mausoleum needs some panache. A body in the basement might be just what the doctor ordered. Remember how many people turned up at the open house we held where that murdered waitress used to live?"

I stared at her. Although I had encountered it before, Margo's tolerance for gore never failed to surprise me. I tended to get woozy when confronted with blood, which Margo found amusing. But she did have a point. "Yes, I do remember. But we don't really know that a body was in the Henstocks' basement at all. It certainly wasn't anywhere in sight when John and I took a look around."

"Don't you let Strutter catch you sayin' that," Margo warned. "As far as she's concerned, she saw a skeleton or a mummy or some other kind of dead body, and you'll never convince her it was a pile of old rags or a discarded Halloween costume." She snorted into the Coke can. "So if we're goin' to get stuck tryin' to sell the Henstock house, a nice, tawdry murder works for me." She changed the subject and handed me the soda. "Seein' Armando tonight, Sugar?"

"Nope. End of the month closing at Telcom. Everybody in the department works late tonight." Armando was the controller of a small, but growing, telecommunications company headquartered in East Hartford. We had met there seven years ago when I managed public and investor relations for the company, and our relationship had endured through my mid-life career crisis. I had spurned my management position to return to my roots as an administrative assistant to a noted Hartford lawyer. That had lasted only a few months, and then I had opened MACK Realty with Margo and Strutter.

"We're having dinner together tomorrow, though, if I can stay awake. He keeps the strangest hours. I'm starving by six o'clock, but he's not ready to eat until about nine. I'm ready for sleep by ten and up again at five-thirty in the morning. He stays up half the night and strolls out to work sometime after nine-thirty." I shook my head.

"It's cultural, Darlin'. He was raised in a hot climate where they take siestas, then eat dinner at some ungodly hour of the night." She waggled her polished fingernails at me for the Coke. "It could work in your favor, though."

"How do you figure that?"

"Think about it. You're worried that after all these years of independence, neither of you is goin' to be able to stand sharin' your space with someone else." Armando and I had been divorced from our respective spouses for a dozen years or more, and both of us had enjoyed our solitude and privacy. "But from what you're tellin' me, you won't actually *be* in the same space a lot of the time during the work week. And you're already used to spendin' the weekends together."

Again, she had a point. We sat in companionable silence. "Interesting day today," I commented after a while. "First Emma leaving, and that weird newspaper clipping. Then that business with the Henstock sisters and a disappearing corpse. If Strutter hadn't seen it too, I'd think the ladies had been into the cooking sherry. By the way, have you ever seen a baby swan?" I told her about the little family Emma and I had seen on the Spring Street Pond. "I'll show you the pictures after I download them tonight. I promised Emma I'd send her updates."

Margo grimaced. "Doesn't sound all that appealin', frankly. Why don't you just keep them for Emma. Will you be all right without your little girl?" Her question was wry, since my little girl was pushing twenty-eight, but her pat on my knee was sympathetic.

"Oh, I'll get by," I assured her. "I just hope she'll have some fun and not study herself into a nervous breakdown or something."

Margo stared at me in disbelief, and we both broke out laughing. There had never been a time when Emma wasn't ready to party, and the chance of her overstudying, I knew well from her high-school years, was slim to none.

"What do you suppose was the matter with Strutter?" I asked, changing the subject once again. "It's not like her to get queasy over a little thing like a corpse."

"Mmmmm," Margo agreed. "And I've seen her digest Jamaican jerk lunches that sent me runnin' for the Tums after just a couple of bites, so I don't think it was indigestion. In fact, I remember her tellin' me once that the only time she had ever lost her breakfast was when she was expectin' Charlie." Charlie was Strutter's twelve-year-old son. We were quiet for a minute, considering. Then we faced each other with open mouths.

"I wonder if she even knows it yet?" I giggled.

"Probably just decidin' when the best time would be to tell her unsuspectin' partners that she's got a bun in the oven," Margo opined. "I want to know if her shiny new husband has been clued in." We exchanged grins, thinking how ecstatic John Putnam would be at the news, though the new couple had been married for less than a year. "Well, at least this day ended up better than it started."

I had to agree. I stuffed the empty Diet Coke can into my voluminous handbag, and we went to fetch Rhett from his luxurious pen. One of the many fat squirrels who routinely raided our trash cans taunted him from a low-hanging tree branch, but Rhett had eyes only for his mistress. I scritched his head, and we parted company for the night.

* * *

As I washed up my few dishes in the kitchen of my condominium a couple of hours later, the events of the day spun through my head. I was usually quite content in my solitude, but tonight I longed for Armando's calm presence. As if he had read my mind, he phoned just as I was drying my hands. "Hi, Handsome. How are things going? Everybody in a bad mood because they have to work late?" I could picture the scene well, as I had lived through it on a monthly basis for several years.

"No worse than usual," he reassured me in his exquisitely accented baritone. "At least the computer system is es-still up and running." Despite his reassuring words, his use of the Spanish "ess" betrayed his fatigue. "How was your day, *Cara?*" Knowing how busy he was, I covered the events of the past twelve hours as succinctly as possible. When I ran down, he chuckled softly. "So just another day at the office, eh? You have been abandoned by your daughter, discovered yet another deceased person, and learned that your dear friend *está en cinta*. It is, how do you say it, the life cycle in a nuthouse."

Since English was not his first language, I usually let Armando's mangled idioms pass, but this time I burst out laughing. "I think you mean nutshell, but in this case, nuthouse is probably more accurate. The inmates were definitely running the asylum for the better part of it. So where are we having dinner tomorrow night?"

"I was hoping for *paella* in your kitchen, after my late night tonight. Would that be all right with you?"

36

A Skeleton in the Closet

I assured him that it would be very all right with me, and he blew me a kiss and disconnected after promising to bring extra shrimp for Jasmine and Simon, my two ancient and very spoiled cats. I knew that Jasmine especially would be as pleased to see Armando as the shrimp, since she had appropriated him as her personal property shortly after Armando and I started seeing each other. I kept telling her that he was too big to be her kitten, but she remained steadfast in her role assignment. Simon, on the other hand, just wolfed down whatever largesse Armando proffered, then returned to my side.

Too wound up to read or sleep, I considered going into my office upstairs and checking my e-mails. Then I remembered the swan pictures on my digital camera and dug it out of my shoulder bag. With the help of the software installed on my computer, it would take only a few minutes to download the best shots, which I could then edit and send electronically to Emma, as promised. I should also send them to myself at the office so that Margo could have a look at the ugly babies tomorrow, although she hadn't been wildly enthusiastic about that idea. Maybe talking about the swan babies would encourage Strutter to confide her news, too.

The first couple of images showed the mature swans clearly, but the cygnets swimming between them were an unrecognizable blur. I had zoomed in for the next shot, focusing on the baby swimming nearest to his dad, and he showed up nicely against the green marsh grasses that tufted behind them. Something blue stuck in the reeds provided further contrast, and I used the cropping and enlarging tools to achieve the clearest possible image.

Pleased with the result, I punched a button and waited for my little HP to grind out a photographic quality print-out. While it did so, I thought about Armando's life-in-a-nuthouse analogy. Idiomatically correct or not, he had certainly gotten that right.

I examined the print-out under my desk lamp and thought about my girl in Boston and my trucker son, driving through the night somewhere out there. *Sleep well, be safe,* I wished them silently. Not knowing exactly why, I peered more closely at the blue flotsam against which the cygnet contrasted so nicely. The material was darker than denim and not so vivid as a royal blue, but so what? It was just a piece of cloth, a rag, much like the one John's flashlight had revealed on the floor of the Henstock girls' basement that morning.

My head swam as I stared, transfixed by what appeared to be a leathery, claw-like hand protruding from the remnants of a dark blue sleeve.

Three

"This absolutely cannot be happening again," I wailed to Margo over the phone the next morning. My shocking discovery of the previous evening had been duly reported to the police, who had promptly dispatched an officer to take my statement and the revealing photograph. According to John Harkness, the mummified remains of a woman, age unspecified, had been retrieved with great difficulty from the marsh surrounding the Spring Street pond at first light this morning. Two officers in a small rowboat had rowed to the site and somehow managed to get a net around the decaying remains, hampered considerably by a large, male swan that flapped his wings threateningly and hissed at them throughout the proceedings. The officers persevered, however, and towed their gruesome bundle to shore, where it was placed in a body bag and transported to the medical examiner's office in Hartford for forensic investigation.

Obviously as sleep-deprived as I was, Margo yawned unabashedly in my ear. "Well, the good news is that Strutter and the Henstock gals have been validated in the eyes of the police. Even John had trouble swallowin' their story about a body in the basement at first, but he stopped scoffin' right quick after he saw that scrawny arm stickin' up out of the grass." She chuckled. "Good thing you noticed it before you emailed that picture off to Emma. Those baby swans were enough to turn her stomach without addin' a decomposin' corpse to the scene."

I winced at Margo's forthright description. "Speaking of Strutter and the Henstocks, do they even know about this development yet?"

"Mmm hmmm. John told Strutter on the phone last night, but he let the ladies sleep through all the hoop-de-doo at the pond this morning, then stopped by to tell them in person. I think he just wanted another cup of Miss Lavinia's tea." I could hear the grin in her voice. "See you later, Sugar."

"Later," I agreed and slouched over to the coffee maker for a refill. At least I'd be able to get a decent night's sleep tonight, I comforted myself. Then I remembered that I'd promised Armando *paella* for dinner. Groaning, I went to check the contents of my pantry cupboard. Rice, chicken stock, saffron, garlic, sweet onions. So far, so good.

I pulled open the refrigerator. Two decent tomatoes and a green pepper. The turkey kielbasa in the meat drawer wasn't chorizo, but it would do. I pulled frozen peas, some chicken, and a a few ciabata rolls out of the freezer to thaw in the refrigerator. It looked as if the shrimp Armando had promised to pick up at City Fish after work would give me the final ingredient. I didn't care for mussels, which were included in most traditional recipes, but Armando and I both preferred shrimp. Jasmine and Simon wouldn't object either, I felt sure. I just hoped I didn't fall dead asleep in my plate. I rinsed out my coffee mug and trudged off to shower and dress.

A Skeleton in the Closet

Arriving at the Law Barn at a little after nine, I found Strutter and Jenny huddled over the mail at the reception desk once again. "Don't tell me. Another clipping? What's this one about ... how women should be seen but not heard?" I waited for a laugh, but I didn't get one.

Jenny held up a second envelope addressed in blue block letters to "Mack Realty," upper and lower case just like the first one. "There's another clipping about that stinky corpse flower getting ready to bloom at the University, but I don't think the quote is from the Bible this time." She handed over a piece of paper to which a clipping from the *Hartford Courant* had been taped. Scrawled in the margin were the words, "The lovesick, the betrayed, and the jealous all smell alike."

"Lovely sentiment, but it doesn't ring a bell." I handed it back and looked at Strutter, who stood silent and frowning. "Mean anything to you?" My casual inquiry produced an explosion.

"Now why would you think that?" she demanded, hands on hips, taking two steps toward me, the better to get in my face. "Was it addressed to me personally? Or are you just assuming someone is making these wild accusations against me?"

I recoiled, eyes wide. "What accusations?" I protested. Then I remembered that Strutter may well be operating under a hormonal handicap. I made a weak stab at defusing her anger. "As far as I can tell so far, these stupid letters aren't directed to anyone in particular. Somebody just thinks we smell bad. Collectively," I added with a smile for good measure and tried to pat her shoulder, but she slid away from me.

"Sorry. Just didn't have my coffee yet. This business with the Henstocks still has my stomach in an uproar." Strutter dropped her eyes and placed one hand over her abdomen, somewhat protectively, I thought. "I've got to get on over to Vista Views anyway. It's my turn to play rental agent this morning." Snatching up her purse and her briefcase, she charged toward the back door of the Law Barn without going anywhere near the coffee pot, I noticed. She nearly ran into Margo, who was just coming in. Jenny and I stared after her.

"What was that all about?" Jenny asked in confusion.

"Yes, what *was* that all about?" Margo agreed, staring after Strutter, "And what's got Strutter all riled up? She about knocked me over."

Jenny and I filled her in on Strutter's reaction to this morning's mail.

"Huh. Seems to me someone is takin' this foolishness a scootch personally, don't you think?" She patted her French twist back into perfection and smoothed her stylish lavender capri outfit unnecessarily. "Now why is that?"

I jerked my eyes meaningfully toward Jenny, who was momentarily distracted by the phone, and headed for the coffee niche. "I haven't got a clue, but until we find out what's going on with her, let's not blow her cover." I poured each of us a mug of fresh brew, which we took down the half-flight to the MACK Realty office. I plunked mine on the desk and booted up the Dell, while Margo arranged herself decoratively on the sofa and checked her cell phone for messages. "It wouldn't be the first time some crackpot decided to distribute a little hate mail."

Margo chuckled, remembering our run-in the previous year with a religious zealot who had harassed the owner of the diner located a few blocks down Old Main Street from our office. "So whatever are we goin' to do about Strutter? If these mood swings get any wilder, we're going to have to keep away from the payin' customers. Why do you suppose she doesn't want to confide in us, her dearest friends in the whole wide world?"

"I have no idea. Maybe it's that old superstition about not telling anyone until you're three months along so you don't have to deal with a lot of questions and drama if you have an early miscarriage." I clicked briskly through my Outlook messages, deleting the garbage emails that grew like mushrooms overnight.

"Seems to me there would be a lot of questions and drama *whenever* you had a miscarriage, so I surely don't understand that one." Margo snapped her cell phone shut and fished in her handbag for a mirror.

"Because miscarriages aren't all that uncommon in the first trimester. After that, the pregnancy is considered well established."

"Well established? Sounds like a vegetable garden or a charitable foundation, not a bun in the oven." She fussed briefly with an imaginary stray lock and dropped her compact back into her purse. "Speakin' of well established, when is that man of yours establishin' himself in your residence? Over the weekend?"

"Monday. It was the only day Armando could get a mover. I think twenty percent of the population chooses June to move. Don't worry, I'll be right here at MACK Realty. This whole moving-in thing is unnerving enough without my having to stand there and watch him invading my space. After work will be soon enough for me to go and survey the wreckage." My stomach did its usual flip-flop at the thought. "I'm really nervous about this."

She chuckled. "No kiddin'. I haven't seen you this het up since ... well, come to think of it, Sugar, since never. What is the worst that could happen? You turn a washer load of his undies pink when your red blouse gets in with them by accident? He leaves the cap off the toothpaste, and you come to blows? What?" She peered at me, obviously perplexed.

I stopped punching keys and returned her gaze. "It's hard to understand, I know. Most women my age would be over the moon to have a wonderful man like Armando in their lives. He's so thoughtful and intelligent and makes me laugh. He's great company. And he doesn't do any of those awful guy things like belching or adjusting himself in public. He's a pack rat, but he's absolutely fastidious about his personal grooming. My kids are fond of him. Jasmine and Simon adore him."

"Not to mention he's cute as the devil." Margo had moved from examining her flawless hair to shaping her already perfect nails with an emery board. "Let's not forget that."

I smiled as I visualized Armando's chiseled profile and coffee-with-cream skin from his toenails to the roots of his hair. "There is that. And he isn't even addicted to televised sports, except for maybe World Cup soccer." I sighed. "It's really not about him. It's about me. I'm the problem."

Another chuckle. "You can be a handful."

I knew that my ex-husband, for one, would be only too happy to agree with Margo. He and I were still excellent friends, but after two children and twenty-two years together, we had had to abandon the idea of living together. Why? I struggled to find the right words.

"For one thing, I'm not what you'd call conventional. I don't care about birthdays, and I don't celebrate most holidays. I don't go to church."

"And how does Armando feel about those things?"

"He's very sentimental. He always makes a big fuss over my birthday, and he loves Christmas. The church thing doesn't bother him, though."

"So let him make a fuss over you once in a while and sing a few Christmas carols. No big deal. What else?"

I searched my mind for other weirdnesses. "The thing is, I'm usually happier alone than I am being with someone else for long periods of time. I'm perfectly content in my own company. I've never been one of those women who can't have a meal in a restaurant or go to a movie by themselves. I do those things all the time very happily. And I like silence. I look forward to coming home to a quiet, orderly house at night and finding things exactly as I left them that morning."

I jumped to my feet and paced in front of the desk, on a roll now. "And I'm selfish, okay? I freely admit it. I want things the way I want them, and I don't enjoy the prospect of making endless compromises to accommodate someone else's preferences. If I want to play rock and roll and bop around my living room, then that's what I do. And if I want to cook fish and cauliflower and eat onions and garlic and drink a little too much wine, well, that's my business." I flapped my hands in frustration. "It's about my personal space. I don't want to lose it. Can you understand this at all?"

Margo gazed at me thoughtfully. "Well, Sugar, remind me never to come to your house for dinner. But the only thing I can't understand is how you managed to hold down demandin' jobs and raise Emma and Joey to be two reasonably socialized adults, considerin' your need for large doses of solitude. Did you always feel that way?"

I thought about it. "Yes. No. Well, not to the same extent, although I was always happy in my own company. As a kid, I lived mostly inside my head, but that changed when the hormones kicked in. I hated school, but I dated and went to dances and fell in love once a week just like most of the other girls. Hell, I was even a cheerleader briefly."

"You were not!" Margo feigned horror, and I paused in my pacing to make a face at her.

"I was too, at least until I quarreled with my boyfriend, who was the captain of the soccer team. He scored a goal during the next game, and it was my turn to do an individual cheer for the scorer. I refused to do it because I was still mad at him, and they kicked me off the squad," I reminisced. Margo threw her head back and howled with laughter.

"Drummed out of the cheerleading squad! Oh, the shame of it."

"And then there was school in Boston, and my first jobs. After that, getting married seemed like a good idea. Wayne and I got along so well, and then Joey and Emma came along, and the days were so full. I always had a full-time job, and there was the house to take care of. Wayne helped when he could, but his job took over his life. Let's face it. I was too tired at the end of each day to think about whether I was happy, whatever that is." I grinned at my friend to lighten my words.

She grinned back, relieved by my attempt at levity. "But then the kids grew up, and you did think about it."

"Yes, I did, more and more as the years went by. When I realized that I no longer wanted to be married, I felt bad, because I knew that would hurt Wayne. So I stuck it out much longer than I probably should have, and when we finally made the break, it was terrible. Still, I knew it was the right thing to do. Wayne deserved to be happy, and so did I." I ran down, remembering the pain of that long-ago time.

"And you have been. Both of you," Margo reminded me gently. She was right. After our divorce, it had taken Wayne only months to meet a terrific woman he would ultimately marry, and the two made a very successful match while I lived, manless, in blissful solitude.

"I didn't even date for more than six years, Margo. Not so much as dinner with a man. I simply wasn't interested."

That got Margo's full attention. "You didn't go out on a date for six years? No handholding, no kissin,' no ..." She wiggled her eyebrows meaningfully.

"No nothing," I said flatly, "and I was perfectly content. If Armando hadn't come straight at me when we both worked at TelCom, I'm quite sure I would have been contentedly celibate to this day."

Margo digested this information in incredulous silence. "Whew, that's some dry spell, Sugar. Thank heaven for Latino cuties who won't take no for an answer."

"He didn't exactly jump me in the office supplies closet. We just happened to hit it off," I frowned and returned to the subject at hand. "The point is, we've been together ever since, and now we're moving in together, and despite months of dithering, I'm still not sure it's a good idea. It's a really big step for me."

"Oh, pooh. It's a really big step for him, too, and you don't see Armando sittin' around wringin' his hands, do you? He's been on his own for years and years too, don't forget. But he's made up his mind that you're the one, and *vice versa*. So just take the plunge and see how it goes. Remember, the movers can get him out of there even quicker than they move him in," she finished lightly. She slumped back on the sofa and resumed filing her nails.

"Maybe that's it. Maybe I just can't face the possibility of having to go through all of that awfulness a second time if this sharing a house thing doesn't work out." I cringed at the thought. "Really. I couldn't."

Margo looked up, understanding at last. "Ahhh. Now I get it." She dropped her nail file back into her capacious purse and leaned forward to grab my hand. "Listen to me. You and Armando are two of the prickliest little devils I've ever met. Total pisspots, the two of you, but somehow you found each other. You know as well as I do, Sugar, that the only thing that matters in a relationship is that you can stand his quirks, and he can stand yours.

You have both had years to decide that you can. I think it's goin' to be just fine."

For Margo, that was quite a speech, and she didn't give speeches very often. "You do?" I asked finally.

"I do," she said firmly, "no pun intended. Now, what can we do to get the knot out of Strutter's tail?"

Four

Twenty minutes later, we decided that since we were just assuming that Strutter was expecting, and it was possible that we were wrong, it was probably best to respect her obvious wish to keep her secret for the time being. We got on with the business of the day. Margo left to show a house, and I went to visit the Henstock ladies to see how they were bearing up under all the excitement.

As I waited once again on the sagging front porch of 185 Broad Street for one of the sisters to answer my knock, I gazed around me and thought how truly splendid the French Second Empire-style house must have been in its heyday. Constructed in the late 1800s by Henstock ancestors, it had been home to Judge and Mrs. Henstock in the early years of their marriage, I knew. I did some hasty calculations and concluded that the sisters, now something over eighty years of age, would have been born in the 1920s. I smiled, imagining the two little girls playing among the now overgrown hedges and shrubbery. Perhaps they had tea parties for their dollies, much like those my Emma had hosted for her Barbies years ago.

A tapping on the front window interrupted my reverie. Lavinia and Ada Henstock peered out at me from the front parlor window. Ada jabbed a finger to her right and mouthed words I couldn't quite make out. Was someone else in the room with them? No, Lavinia wanted me to go somewhere. But where? Then I remembered the side entrance and nodded to show I understood. She smiled, and the sisters trotted out of sight to let me in.

Later, seated at the capacious kitchen table with another cup of excellent tea before me, I broached the subject of the remains retrieved that morning from the Spring Street Pond. "You've had quite a couple of days, haven't you?"

Ada rolled her eyes in agreement and sipped thirstily at her tea, but to my surprise, Lavinia's eyes gleamed with excitement. "Oh, my, yes! Such a lot of coming and going, what with the plumber and you and your partners, and then the police. That nice Lieutenant came by again this morning to give us the news about finding the, um, body." She slid her eyes sideways to Ada, but receiving no rebuke for her boldness, she continued. "I don't suppose we've had this many people in the house since poor Papa's funeral. My, wasn't that a day, though." Her face glowed at the memory.

Mention of the corpse hadn't drawn a response from Ada, but mention of their father's demise did. "For heaven's sake, Lavinia, that was nearly forty years ago. We have certainly entertained guests since then. Why, don't you remember that Christmas open house we had in celebration of the Bicentennial in '96?" She was positively bristling at the implication that she and her sister were antisocial.

"I'm sure it was a lovely occasion," I intervened hastily. "Tell me, have you had any further thoughts on the identity of the body? I'm sure the police have already questioned you about that, but I confess that I'm curious."

"Mmmm, yes, we have." Ada stirred her tea thoughtfully. At first, we thought it might be from the Civil War era, perhaps a runaway slave who had been hidden here by one of our ancestors. That would have been just like a Henstock. The Underground Railroad was quite active in these parts, you know."

I hadn't known, but I was appropriately impressed.

"But it wasn't a slave, no," Lavinia chimed in. "The authorities who first viewed the remains were quite clear about that, the Lieutenant told us. Not old enough, and that blue fabric she was wearing was certainly not Civil War era."

I was becoming interested in spite of my vow not to get caught up in another intrigue. "They know for certain it was a woman?"

"Oh, yes, Dear. But as I say, she was of much more recent vintage than the Civil War. World War II perhaps."

"Don't speak of the wretched woman as if she were a bottle of Papa's claret, Lavinia!" Ada tsk-ed her sister and made an effort to mask her irritation. "All we know is it's a woman who must have died sometime after 1945."

"Goodness! However did they date the remains that quickly?" I couldn't help but ask.

"Oh, it had nothing to do with the body," Lavinia assured me. "Much too soon for that. But Ada and I did some research last night in Papa's ledgers and so on, and we founds records showing that that old closet in the basement had been constructed in 1945. So the body couldn't have been hidden there before that time. It was right there in Papa's handwriting. He was so meticulous about his papers," she concluded with satisfaction. Ada nodded wearily in agreement, and my heart went out to her. Both sisters must be exhausted after the doings of the past twenty-four hours, but Ada seemed to be the only one feeling the strain. Lavinia appeared to be thriving on the unexpected excitement.

"Why was the closet or whatever you want to call that enclosure next to the furnace built in the first place?" I couldn't help but ask. "It seems only logical that those pipes would have needed maintenance from time to time, and it must have been very inconvenient to have them right next to a brick wall. By the way, was there a door to the closet? It was so demolished, I couldn't tell."

Ada paused mid-sip to consider my question and knit her brows in consternation. "Why, I don't recall, do you, Sister? We were young women at that time, and the house always seemed to be full of workers of one sort or another and people from dear Papa's office. I can't say I ever paid any of them much attention."

Lavinia explained more fully. "Our mother died when Ada and I were just girls. Influenza took her when we were nine and ten years old, and Papa was just devastated. For simply years, he spent every evening alone in his study, lost in his work. I believe he just about forgot he had children, he was so sorrowful about losing precious Mama. If it hadn't been for Clara and Agnes …"

"… the cook and the housekeeper who came to live with us after Mama's death," Ada interjected.

"… we probably would have gone off to school looking like ragamuffins," Lavinia continued without missing a beat. "But those two good ladies saw to it that we were properly turned out for every occasion. And there was always bread and jam and cold milk after school. Why, we would sit right here at this very table, chattering about our day, while Clara got the supper started and Agnes oversaw our homework. How I miss those dear souls." A misty smile played about her mouth as she recalled her old friends.

Ada brought her sharply back to the question at hand. "Yes, they were wonderful to us, Dear, but that doesn't get us any closer to knowing why that closet was built ten years later. Do you have any ideas, Lavinia? It might shed some light on who that poor woman was." She shuddered. "To think that we have been living all these years with that dreadful ... thing ... right under our feet the whole time."

Reluctantly, Lavinia dragged herself away from her childhood memories and gave Ada's question her attention. "Why, yes, I believe I do," was her surprising response. "At least, I know what Papa said it was for at the time." A sly smile played with the corners of her mouth. Judging from Ada's expression, the implication that the Judge may have invented a cover story was not lost on her, although I pretended not to notice. "Whatever do you mean, Sister? It seems odd that Papa would have told you about this and not me, and I don't remember anything."

"Oh, you were far too taken with young Robert Sloane and your parties and dances and tennis games to be aware of anything as mundane as a closet being constructed in the basement. Ada was always the social butterfly, far prettier than I was," Lavinia confided, and

Ada colored. "It was for his personal papers, Papa said, so they could be locked up away from prying eyes. A vault, I guess you'd call it. He had letters and diaries and trial records of cases dating back to the beginning of his career as a lawyer... oh, all sorts of things. He always said he would write his memoirs when he retired from the bench, but in the meantime, he wanted to protect the innocent. At least, that's what he said." Again, I ignored the implication of her words.

"But surely those things would be kept in his study or a file cabinet or something," I said. "Whose prying eyes did he mean?"

"I assumed at the time that he meant Clara and Agnes, which was complete nonsense. My goodness, they would never pry. But now, I'm not so sure that was it."

It was Ada's turn to question her sister. "What do you mean, Lavinia? For heaven's sake, just spit it out!"

Lavinia regarded her for a moment before deciding to answer. "I think he meant us. Now I think he built that closet to lock those papers away from us. As children, we wouldn't have been the least bit interested in looking at his old files, and we wouldn't have understood anything in them even if we had snooped through them. But as young women ..." she shrugged.

Ada stared at her sister, clearly confounded. "If I'm understanding you correctly, Lavinia, our father, a grieving widower and a respected member of this community for decades, had secrets to keep. Whether they were his or other people's, we don't know, but he was certainly determined to keep them."

"But wouldn't any closet with a lock on the door have been sufficient?" I was still mystified by the enclosure in the basement.

"I guess that would depend on how big the secrets were … and about whom," Lavinia commented, doing more damage to her image as a doddering airhead. I was beginning to suspect that had been carefully cultivated over the years as protective coloration. Nobody expected much of a ditz, especially when she had an exceptionally capable, not to say domineering, older sister to manage things. She shifted her gaze pointedly from Ada to me and then back again.

Ada addressed her sister. "Lavinia, Mrs. Lawrence is here to help us resolve this dreadful situation. If you know something that might help us do that, just go ahead and tell us. It has been my experience that secrets always come out sooner or later anyway, and Mrs. Lawrence can be trusted with ours, isn't that right?" She looked at me for confirmation, and I nodded mutely. As a rule, I hated being the repository of other people's secrets, but this time, I had an avid interest in what Lavinia might have to say. "There now. What more can you tell us?"

Lavinia rose to replenish the teapot, whether to hide her face or give herself time to choose her words, I couldn't be sure. Her hand trembled as she poured more hot water over the tea ball inside the pot, and she replaced the lid carefully before turning back to us.

"For one thing, Papa wasn't quite the grieving widower you remember, Ada. Oh, for a few years, perhaps, when we were still young. It was only decent in those days that a few years elapsed between our mother's death and, well, Papa's renewed interest in socializing."

"Renewed interest in … oh, do stop pussyfooting around, Lavinia. Say what you mean!"

"Women," Lavinia said firmly. "Rather a lot of them, as I recall. You were always out and about with one or another of your young men, but I spent a lot of evenings right here in this house with little to amuse me but the comings and goings of Papa's, um, guests."

At this, my eyebrows climbed higher than Ada's, but I kept silent.

"Do you mean that Papa entertained lady friends right here in the house, and I didn't know about it?"

"As I said, Dear, you were preoccupied, and Papa's visitors usually arrived after you had gone out for the evening and Clara and Agnes had retired to their rooms on the third floor. Came to the side entrance and left the same way through the kitchen after spending several hours with Papa in his study. He always told me they were clients, but if that were true, why did he keep his study door locked, I wonder?"

Ada placed her teacup carefully in its saucer and clasped her hands on top of the table for support. "What makes you believe that he locked it?"

"I tapped on his door one evening to see if he and his, er, client would like some tea. He didn't answer, and when I turned the knob to poke my head in, it was locked. I took my own tea straight up to my bedroom, and the next morning, neither Papa nor I mentioned it. It was right after that when he arranged to have the vault built in the basement."

I didn't dare look at Ada and busied myself pouring more tea.

"And you never mentioned any of this to me," Ada said. "Why not?"

"Why, I suppose because it stopped," Lavinia stated flatly. "All of it, the women and the late-night visits and the closed-door meetings just stopped. I never knew Papa to see a woman socially again, in this house or elsewhere, until the day he died. And after a few years, I decided I must have been mistaken, and the whole matter left my mind. Until now," she added.

I cleared my throat. "When did the Judge pass away? I know he had a long and distinguished career on the bench."

The ladies consulted each other silently. "It was the year that nice Mr. Kennedy was assassinated," Lavinia asserted.

"The President was assassinated in 1963," I said.

"Not President Kennedy, the other one, the brother," Ada put forward. "It was at that hotel in California. Bobby, I believe it was, which I always thought was a rather silly name for a grown man, and him the Attorney General."

"Then that would be 1968," I said, conveying another of the few dates I had managed to retain from my barely read school textbooks. "The Judge must have been in his sixties by then and ready to retire, but he never got around to writing his memoir?"

"No," Lavinia confirmed sadly. "He died at the bench. Right in the middle of the prosecutor's summation,

Papa suffered a massive heart attack and fell over dead. It was in all the papers."

I could well imagine that it had been. "So that closet or vault was opened after his death?"

"No, it wasn't," Ada spoke up at last. "I'm quite sure I would have remembered that, wouldn't you, Lavinia?"

"Oh, yes. It would have been quite a noisy business, having to break down the door. There's no question that we would have known about it. In fact, we would have had to arrange to have it done, but we didn't. Quite frankly, I had forgotten all about it by that time."

I carefully swallowed a sip of tea, then asked the questions that were front and center in all of our minds, "So how did that woman's body get put into the vault, and what happened to your father's private papers?"

* * *

"What did the ladies have to say then?" Armando prompted me that evening, as fascinated by my report of the conversation as I had been by the real thing. While our paella baked in the oven, we sat in our customary spots, side-by-side on the living room sofa, sipping a shiraz we had both come to enjoy. A small fire enlivened the hearth and brightened the evening, which had turned cool and rainy. Having cadged as many shrimp as they figured they could get, Jasmine and Simon lay on their cushion before the cozy blaze. As usual, fourteen-pound Simon's head lolled on seven-pound Jasmine's belly, which she tolerated for the warmth.

"Nothing. We all just sat there and looked at each other for a minute. Then Ada had the bright idea of trying to contact Clara and Agnes to see if they could shed any light on what had happened to that vault and the papers inside it, but Lavinia reminded her that Clara had passed away long since, and Agnes, if she's still alive, must be well into her nineties and more than a little forgetful. We agreed that they would do what they could to locate her on the off chance that she might remember something happening around the time of the Judge's death. The poor old girls are desperate to get this thing resolved so they can repair their leaking pipes and get that aging white elephant on the market." I shook my head in despair. "I can't imagine who would buy it, though. It's in such disrepair, and it's so big. There must be eight or nine bedrooms ..." Suddenly, the beginning of an idea about who might buy the Henstocks' house and for what purpose formed in my head, but I kept silent.

A small log broke in the grate and showered sparks into the ashes below. Armando rose to add more wood. "How is it that you get yourself in the middle of these intrigues, *Mia*?" he asked, poking at the embers carefully so as not to disturb the slumbering felines. "You are becoming like that lady on television who lives in Maine and writes murder stories. Soon you will be banned from people's houses because they fear you will discover a body under the bed."

I was not amused. "I do not, as you put it, 'get myself in the middle' of these things, and I'm not in the habit of poking around underneath people's beds. Frankly, until I went into the residential realty business, I had no idea how many family intrigues there appear to be swirling around in a small town at any given time. The skeleton in the Henstock sisters' closet happened to be literal, but there are plenty of the figurative variety to go around, believe me. Sometimes it seems as if everyone has something to hide, and as soon as we list a house for sale, some secret pops out into the open to complicate matters."

Armando closed the firescreen doors and reseated himself next to me. "Perhaps that is because one often buys a house because of a marriage or a birth, and then sells a house because of a divorce or a death. These are momentous occasions spurred by very strong emotions. Love, jealousy, sorrow, anger are all very powerful. You know that."

As was often the case, his observation was right on the money, but I wasn't about to say so. His implication that I somehow inserted myself into other people's family imbroglios still rankled. "And what are your secrets, Armando? Now that we're moving in together, am I going to discover something sinister about your past?" I draped my legs across his lap and put my arms around his neck. "What is the skeleton in your closet?" I asked the question lightly, but I was half serious. They say you can't really know anybody else until you share a roof.

As usual when he was directly questioned, Armando took evasive action. "I could ask the same of you, could I not?" he countered smilingly. "The difference between us is that I would never do that. Your past belongs to you only, and it does not matter to me. It is today and tomorrow that I wish to share with you." And that unsatisfactory answer was clearly all I was going to get. I uncoiled myself and got up to serve the paella, cursing Latino men's passion for privacy under my breath.

Much later, we dozed together on the sofa while we watched the fire die and settle. A knitted afghan warded off the evening chill, as did the two cats, who had recognized a better heat source when they saw it and abandoned the hearth to pile on top of us. "What's the schedule for Monday? Are the movers coming to your apartment first thing in the morning?"

"Yes, mine is the first move of the day. All my belongings will be here by noon. I am sure you will have a heart attack when you come in the door after work. There will be boxes piled in the hallway, suitcases all over, my bed probably stuck halfway up the stairs …"

"That's not funny." He knew how I felt about clutter and disorder and how much I dreaded the inevitable mess of his moving in. Some things we were very clear about. For one thing, we had decided that having separate bedrooms and bathrooms would give each of us some private space, much needed at our ages. As attracted as we were to each other, we weren't a pair of hormone-crazed twenty-somethings. Both of us had been married before, and both of us had enjoyed more than ten years of independence. This sharing of space was going to take some getting used to.

Besides, we functioned on drastically different internal clocks. I was up at five-thirty a.m. and out the door to work by seven-thirty. He arose at eight and got to his desk at a leisurely ten a.m. At the other end of the day, I was home by six p.m. and in bed with a crossword puzzle by nine-thirty. He rarely appeared before eight and was a true night owl, up until the wee hours. For this reason, I had had the wall between the living room and my bedroom soundproofed so he could watch television without disturbing me.

A large upstairs bedroom, which had always been empty, awaited him, as did the adjoining bathroom. Previously, these rooms had been used only by Joey on his once-a-week overnight stays and the occasional visitor. The large loft area that overlooked the living room where we sat would become Armando's home office. Mine would remain in the small guest bedroom directly over my bedroom/bathroom suite on the first floor. Once we got past the moving-in stage, it really should work, so why was I still so doubtful?

"Where will your son be spending his Monday nights after this?" Armando asked, distracting me from the worries that scurried through my head.

"With his father or friends, or maybe in a nice motel. He doesn't have apartment rent to pay, so I'm sure he'll be fine." I remembered the telephone conversation of a few weeks ago when I had broken the news to Joey about Armando's and my plans. "Whatever he chooses to do, he was absolutely fine with the news. As a matter of fact, I got the distinct impression that he was finding the weekly visits to Mom a little confining and was glad to be let off the hook."

I could feel Armando smiling. "He has a new lady friend, perhaps?"

"Always. I've just never known it to be the same one two weeks running."

"And why should it be? He is still at an age where he can afford to enjoy himself."

"What's that supposed to mean? That you're not having any fun?" I flared.

Armando sat up, dislodging the cats. They lumped off the sofa and flopped down on the rug to groom themselves with elaborate indifference, their backs pointedly to us. Gently, Armando took me by the shoulders. "Do not be so quick to take offense. It will be all right, *Mia*. We will survive this change, even enjoy it. It is the right thing to do. It is time."

For both our sakes, I hoped he was right.

Five

Saturday morning evaporated in the usual marathon of housework, laundry, grocery shopping and other errands that piled up during the workweek. The cool rain continued, and I stopped by the Spring Street Pond to check on the cygnets and take the weekly update photos I had promised Emma. Because of the weather, I had the muddy street to myself. I put down the passenger side window and peered out into the reeds, trying to spot the white feathers of the huge cob. The water was high, rushing a full inch over the spillway and into the culvert running beneath the road, but no birds were in sight. Mom and dad were probably huddled over their scrawny, featherless brood in an effort to keep them dry and generate some warmth, I reasoned. After a few more minutes, I put up the window and pulled out my cell phone to report to Emma.

"How's it going, Em?" I asked when she answered, her voice fogged with sleep although it was after noon. "Is it as rainy there as it is here?"

"Mmm-hmm. A good day for sleeping. Thank God even crummy hotel rooms come with coffeemakers these days." Water ran in the background. "So what's happening with you? Same old, same old?"

By the time I finished a five-minute rundown on the Henstock ladies' skeleton, the retrieval of the remains from the pond, the probability that Strutter was with child, and Armando's and my imminent cohabitation, Emma sounded fully alert. "Whoa, I can't believe what's been going on there, and I've only been in Boston a few days."

I agreed that it had been an eventful time and promised to keep her posted. More awake now, she filled me in briefly on her classes and textbooks, as well as her fellow students. "How are the swans doing?"

"Funny you should ask. I've been parked next to the pond for fifteen minutes now, and I haven't seen a feather, but I wouldn't expect to in this weather. The babies can't stay warm and dry without their adult feathers, and those are a few weeks off yet."

"Can you hang on a sec, 'Cita?" She covered her cell phone briefly, and there was muffled conversation in the background. "Sorry, Momma. Ron's here." She paused. "You're okay with that information, right?"

"Considering my upcoming living arrangements, I could hardly be otherwise without being a huge hypocrite," I pointed out. "The fact that you're nearly thirty, not sixteen, helps, too."

"Hard to believe, isn't it?" I heard the smile in her voice as she teased me.

"Except when I look in the mirror. Well, I'm glad you have company, Dearie. I'll keep you posted on developments here. Say hello to Officer Ron. Oh! Before I go, have you talked to your brother lately?"

"Now that you mention it, no, I haven't. His schedule is so crazy, and I've been up here, but I figured we'd talk at some point when things settle down a little. How is he taking being thrown out of the nest? Things going okay with his new girlfriend, or has she already bitten the dust?"

"I can't really say, because I haven't heard from him in more than a week either. New girlfriend? Hmmm. Maybe Armando was right." I repeated what he had said about Joey's not being upset with our new arrangement.

"Interesting! I'll definitely give him a call sometime this weekend and get back to you. Don't you worry. I'll drag it out of him."

We disconnected, and on impulse, I punched in Joey's cell phone number. As usual of late, my call went right to voice mail. "Remember me, your mother? Just because we aren't roommates any longer doesn't mean you need to be a stranger. Call me."

I hung up and resumed my surveillance of the pond. Nothing. A beat-up black van pulled up behind me, engine idling. Another birdwatcher, I assumed, or one of the locals who used the area for a lunch break. The pond was a regular stop for many of the town's residents, especially on the weekend. I sighed and started the engine.

My conversation with Emma hadn't comforted me as much as I had hoped. I still felt very unsettled. *Too many changes*, I speculated. I had always handled change poorly, preferring an orderly structure within which to live out my days, but over the last couple of years, I had experienced nothing but change, not to mention the two murders I had found myself involved in solving. My score on the life stress scale would be off the chart, and still, the changes kept coming. Starting MACK Realty with Margo and Strutter, Armando moving in, Emma off to Boston,

Joey totally on his own and suddenly silent – and oh, yes, another mysterious body cropping up on the premises of one of our listings. Wherever the swans were today, I envied them the regular seasons of their lives. Then I remembered that they raised between three and seven offspring a year, every year, and I reconsidered.

I stopped for a red light at the intersection of Maple Street and the Silas Deane Highway and glanced in my rearview mirror. To my surprise, the black van I had noticed at the pond was behind me. Well, not so surprising, really. Maple and the Deane were two of the major thoroughfares in Wethersfield and were heavily traveled by local residents and drivers en route from Glastonbury to Newington, as well.

The fact was that I had been particularly watchful of vehicles that seemed to be shadowing me since an incident a year or so ago. At that time, a black Trans Am, driven by an unbalanced man who believed he was protecting a lady friend, had harassed me all the way from Wethersfield to Glastonbury, attempting to force me off the road. After a hair-raising, ten-minute chase across the Putnam Bridge, I wound up churning across the front lawn of the Glastonbury Police Department, where a nice young officer discovered me having hysterics a moment later. Ever since, I had been wary.

The light changed, and I pulled across the highway and around the long curve of Maple, then turned right on Prospect. The van stayed with me up and down the series of grades as Prospect crossed Wolcott Hill, then Ridge Road. When I signaled for the right turn into The Birches,

I half expected the van to follow, but it continued straight on Prospect.

I shook off my apprehension as I proceeded down the entrance road at the posted fifteen m.p.h. limit. By the time I reached my driveway, the van was nowhere in sight, and my heartbeat slowed as I pushed the garage door opener on my visor. As soon as I pulled inside, I shut the door again and let relief wash through me. What was my problem? All at once, having a man around the house seemed like a great idea.

It took two trips up the garage stairs into the kitchen to wrestle in all of the groceries, dry cleaning, and drugstore purchases. I hardly spent a penny all week, but on Saturday, the cash outlay was impressive. It would be nice to be sharing some of the household expenses, too, I admitted. Come this time next week, Armando would be living here. I wondered how that would feel. Would he come with me on my round of errands?

I chuckled as I remembered a couple Armando and I had seen once at the supermarket. A thin, scowling woman pushed a cart alongside the meat case. Clearly out of patience, she looked back over her shoulder at a sulky fellow lingering in the soup aisle. "Richard, are you or are you not going to participate?" the woman shrilled. Richard put down his minestrone and slouched to her side, and Armando and I couldn't help but snicker. Now, whenever Armando dragged his feet about something, I would put my hands on my hips and bark, "Armando, are you or are you not going to participate?" It never really worked, of course, but it always gave us a laugh.

Jasmine yawned her way into the kitchen and stuck her head into one bag after another, her nose telling her there was fresh ground meat in there somewhere. "Yes, you're right," I applauded the old lady. I pulled out a package of lean beef and broke her off a chunk before rewrapping it in meal-sized portions for the freezer. She was lucky this time and swallowed the last morsel before Simon's nose kicked in, and he appeared in the doorway. She sashayed past him nonchalantly and leaped up onto the living room sofa to clean her whiskers. Simon eyed me suspiciously. "Oh, all right, you win." I opened one of my freezer bags and gave him just a bite. Satisfied, he trailed after Jasmine and jumped up on the sofa to snuggle against her.

On impulse I climbed the stairs to the second floor to have a last look around before move-in day. The large spare room had been freshly painted and the carpeting steam-cleaned. The closet was empty, and the walls were bare. How different it would look with all of Armando's things inside. I knew that he was a packrat who hated to part with anything, and whatever furniture he had would be bursting with books and art supplies, magazines and papers. I also knew that his favorite place to store things was the floor and that every surface would be covered with books and papers to keep them close at hand. I thought of poor Grace, my once-a-month cleaning person, attempting to deal with this room. It might be time to give her a raise.

Wandering across the loft area that overlooked the living room below, I stuck my head into the large bathroom. A new cabinet occupied a niche behind the shower/tub combination, and another one hung on the wall next to the commode. Fresh towels hung on the rods. The mirror shone, and a new shower curtain hung from the rod. Everything was ready ... except me. I wondered how long it would take me to adjust to this new arrangement. I was happy about it, I reminded myself. Really, I was. Living under the same roof would take our relationship to a whole new level, I felt sure. But I remembered how crowded I had felt by my first marriage and how much I had loved the last dozen years of peaceful solitude. Was I too old a leopard to change my spots?

Armando was devoting his weekend to sorting and packing his belongings in preparation for Monday's move, a task I was thankful to be spared. I took advantage of his absence Saturday evening to get in some quality girl time with such activities as coloring my hair, touching up my nails and giving myself a pedicure.

I chatted with Armando briefly about halfway through my manicure, then checked my office voicemail and emails while my toenails dried. Margo would be spending the evening with John, I knew, and Strutter ... frankly, I didn't know what to do about Strutter. If she was pregnant, why wouldn't she confide in us? And if she wasn't, then what on earth was the matter with her? Of the three of us, it was always Strutter who was the *de facto* mom. She was a strong, centered, loving woman with uncommonly good sense and enormous tact. It was she upon whom we relied for sound advice, and in this situation, I could really use some. Unfortunately, I couldn't ask Strutter for it.

By nine p.m. I was sitting in front of the living room television pressing buttons at random on the remote control. For the umpteenth time I wondered how it was possible to have more than one hundred channels at my disposal but find nothing I wanted to watch. I was cheered briefly by a PBS special on James Taylor, one of my personal favorites; but as usual, ten minutes into the show, it was interrupted by a fundraising break. *Commercial-free television, phooey,* I thought bitterly and punched the television off. The silence was a blessed relief from the pitchman's yammering.

I leaned my head back against the sofa and turned out the light next to me, the better to enjoy the silence. Jasmine and Simon, unaccustomed to my company on a Saturday night, were packed on either side of me, and I soon found my eyelids drooping.

With a start, I lurched out of my doze and wondered what had awakened me. The phone wasn't ringing, but I realized that my heart was beating fast. The little hairs on the back of my neck were prickling an atavistic warning. I put my feet on the floor and listened intently. Hot water heater humming in the basement. Refrigerator motor. And a soft knocking on the front door. Knock knock knock, three times, almost furtive-sounding. Hesitantly, I walked down the hall in bare feet and put my eye to the peephole in the front door. The porch light was on. A man stood on the front porch with his back to me. Dark blue windbreaker, shaven head, jeans, running shoes of some sort. Hands jammed deeply into his pockets.

I considered opening the door until I spotted the van in my driveway. Black, like the one that had been behind me on the road earlier. Instinctively, I drew back from the door and made my way soundlessly back into the living room, where I picked up the wireless phone, heart pounding.

Thus armed for an emergency call to 911, if necessary, I tiptoed back down the hallway and up the three steps to the staircase landing. From the window there, I would have a clear view of the front porch and the driveway. I stood well to one side of the window and peeked cautiously through the slats of the vertical blinds. The porch was empty, but the van remained in the driveway. Where was the driver, and why was that van on my property at ten-thirty on a Saturday night?

I sat down on the landing to ponder that question. Then I heard it—the sound of someone trying to turn the knob on the door at the back of the house. It led from the deck to the living room, and I wasn't at all sure that it was locked. Years before, I had applied a window decal from Radio Shack proclaiming that this house was protected by the XYZ Security System or some such, but I was sure that wouldn't fool anyone but an unsophisticated teenager.

The living room drapes were wide open, so the intruder knew full well from the blazing lights and the pedicure paraphernalia that I was at home. I drew more deeply into the shadows of the staircase landing and tried to think clearly. I could dial 911 and have the Wethersfield police here within minutes, or I could lock myself into an upstairs bedroom with the phone and attempt to get a handle on the intruder's intentions. To my own amazement, I opted to do the latter.

The doorknob stopped rattling, and as relieved as I was to realize that it must indeed be locked, I knew I had only seconds to get a second look at Van Man before he left the deck. I flew up the remaining stairs into what soon would be Armando's bedroom and dropped to my hands and knees to scrabble across the carpet below window height. Again keeping well to one side, I peered between the blinds down to the deck below. Nothing. Damn! I had missed him again. I held my breath and listened for whatever clues the house could give me about my visitor's next move. If he broke a window pane, I would lock myself into the bedroom and punch in 911.

All was silent for a full minute. I tiptoed warily to the door of the bedroom and stopped to listen again, every sense straining. Another minute and I heard the unmistakable sound of the van's engine turning over. Racing back down the stairs to the landing, I was just in time to see the van back quietly out of my driveway and move slowly, slowly down The Birches' access road to Prospect Street. I couldn't see the license plate, but I noted that the plastic cover on one of the rear lights was broken.

I sat down on the landing to try to make sense of this strange visitation. Should I call 911 and report the attempted intrusion? Or was it an attempted intrusion at all? The man had rattled the back doorknob. Maybe he was a neighbor attempting to stick a UPS package that had been wrongly delivered to him in my door. That could also explain why he had been driving the van in this neighborhood earlier in the day, if indeed it was the same van. That could just be my paranoia working overtime.

A Skeleton in the Closet

Could the man have something to do with those crazy letters we had been receiving at MACK Realty about the stink of abomination or whatever the writer had been raving about? Those letters had seemed to be directed at all of us generally, and this man was following only me, if in fact he was following anybody. Could my visitor be involved in whatever was happening at the Henstocks' house? Again, all of us had been in and out of the house in the last few days, so why was I being singled out?

My feet were cold. I got up and returned to the living room sofa, although not before drawing the drapes tightly shut and turning on the floodlights over the back deck to discourage a repeat visit. Jasmine and Simon had altered their positions just far enough to glean maximum warmth from each other, since I had abandoned them. It was odd that the presence of a stranger on the back deck had apparently bothered them not at all. I pulled the afghan over me and resumed my musings.

The only thing I felt fairly certain of was that the van in my driveway tonight had been the same one behind me on the road this afternoon. I couldn't explain to myself why I believed that. It was just a gut feeling. I hadn't seen the license plate earlier, nor the broken taillight cover. I hadn't been able to see the driver, because the windshield was heavily tinted – more heavily than the law allowed, if I didn't miss my guess. That left only instinct to guide me, but my instinct was screaming that the man standing on my front porch this evening was the driver of the van behind me this afternoon. Assuming that was true, what could I logically do with this information? Call the police? And report what ... that a man I didn't know had rattled my back doorknob, and he was driving a dark-colored van with a broken taillight cover?

Briefly, I considered getting Armando's advice, then discarded the idea. If I had learned anything about Armando, it was not to raise the alarm with him unless it was absolutely necessary. All I had to do was tell him some strange man was rattling my back doorknob, and he'd be having a *bona fide* security system installed in the condo tomorrow morning. No, I decided. Margo was the best one to consult on this. Southern belle she might be, but she could be counted upon not to overreact.

* * *

Twenty minutes after calling Margo, I found myself brewing coffee for the half-dozen people who now occupied my house. Margo and a young officer from the Wethersfield Police Department rattled around upstairs, checking windows and looking in closets to be sure no intruder lurked in the shadows, which I found a bit over the top. John Harkness stood in the living room barking orders into the telephone. Two additional officers, who had screeched into my driveway in a cruiser, lights blazing, were patrolling the outside circumference of the house for signs of attempted entry. And Mary Feeney, my elderly and eccentric next-door neighbor, sat in my kitchen, agog with interest.

At something more than eighty years of age, Mary had retired more than a decade ago and now spent her time annoying The Birches' property manager by committing minor infractions of the association rules, zooming around town in her disreputable and ancient blue

Chevy, and enjoying an unlikely dalliance with my neighbor on the other side, Roger Peterson.

"Wow, with all of this hubbub, I thought you'd been strangled or knifed or at least were being held hostage," she commented, eyes glittering with excitement behind thick spectacles. "We haven't had this much hoo-ha since the water main broke a year ago last winter, remember, Kiddo?" I remembered it well, it having been the trigger for a serious quarrel between Armando and me.

"Sorry to disappoint you," I said dryly, "but I'm alive and well and not being held at gunpoint just at the moment." I transferred mugs from a cupboard onto a tray and added the sugar bowl and a small pitcher of milk.

"Yeah, well, I sure thought you must be in big trouble, what with that police cruiser and all these good-looking young fellas in uniform prowling around in the bushes." Mary jumped up to pour herself some coffee, then looked around. "This sure would be better with a shot of bourbon in it, and I'm not on duty like those cops skulking around your yard. Got any?"

Resignedly, I fished the Jim Beam out of a lower cupboard. I added a generous dollop to her proffered mug, then shrugged and put a splash into my own. Maybe the alcohol would offset the caffeine, and I'd be able to sleep once all of these people went away, I reasoned. I carried the tray into the living room, Mary trotting behind me, and plunked it onto the coffee table in front of Margo.

"I should have known better than to call you about something like this when you were with Lieutenant Hardnose here," I sulked at her. "The idea was to *avoid* creating a scene like this, all totally unnecessary and a complete waste of the taxpayers' money." Rebelliously, I plopped into the double recliner and took a big swig of my doctored brew. Mary eeled into the seat next to me, clutching her mug to her scrawny chest.

Margo grinned, refusing to take the bait. "Now you know perfectly well that John wasn't about to take any chances with the safety of my very dearest friend. Besides, I'm the one who should be poutin', don't you think? It was my Saturday evenin' ruined by whoever that nasty man was givin' you the willies." She gazed adoringly at John Harkness, who finished his call and charged out the back door to supervise his subordinates' search of the back yard and adjacent marsh.

"I don't know why they're doing all this," I sighed. "As I told the officer who arrived first, the nasty man, as you put it, was long gone before I called you."

"Yes," said John, reappearing through the back door, but under the circumstances, it's not out of the realm of probability that he would come back, and this time, he might be on foot. The entire perimeter of The Birches is woods and marsh, as you know, and that would be great cover for somebody wanting to conceal himself. Best to be on the safe side."

I handed him a mug of coffee *sans* bourbon. If he was going to get all official on me, I could play by the rules, too. Margo patted the seat next to her invitingly, and he obediently went to join her.

"I can't imagine why anyone would want to go to all that trouble. That marsh is too soggy for anyone but the critters, and the mosquitoes are fearsome at this time of night. I can't imagine why this man was here *at all*, frankly, so I simply don't know what else to tell you." I had already given a minute-by-minute account of the incident to a young officer who had arrived in a cruiser.

"Well, let's put our heads together, and maybe we can come up with something." John jumped up again and stuck his head back out the door and spoke briefly to an officer on the deck. Within seconds, the squad of investigators evaporated into the night, taking the noise of their walkie-talkies with them. I noticed that John left the back floodlights on when he resumed his seat.

Mary piped up again. "All I know is that I was watching a rerun of "Saturday Night Live" in my living room with Roger when all hell broke loose ..." She gasped and put one hand over her mouth, eyes wide, and scrambled to her feet. "Roger! I forgot all about him in the excitement. Sorry, but I've got to scoot." And she was gone, moving faster than I would have thought possible for a woman of her age.

I rolled my eyes at Margo, who was familiar with Mary's quirks, and gave John my attention. "Okay, what do you need to know?"

* * *

Half an hour later, we had reviewed everything we knew about the skeleton found in the Henstocks' basement and could find absolutely no connection to that case and the man who appeared to be following me. Then Margo remembered the nasty mailings we had been receiving at MACK Realty from another person unknown. John perked up and sat forward as she described the two clippings we had gotten to date.

"The writer uses words like 'fornication,'" she elaborated. "That sounds like some sort of religious zealot to me. And the clippin' was about that big, stinky flower they're cultivatin' up at the University of Connecticut, which looks like some sort of phallic symbol to me."

"But then, so many things do," I couldn't help from commenting. I noticed that John's mouth twitched in that way he had when he was amused but too gentlemanly to let it show.

Instead, he commented diplomatically, "I think you might be right about the religious nut. Hard to say if it's a man or a woman, but the handwriting may give us a clue."

"I don't think you could call it handwritin' exactly," Margo mused. "More like big block printin' in some kind of marker. Blue, I think it was." I nodded in agreement.

"Let me have a look at those letters. You do still have them, right?"

Margo and I looked at each other, trying to remember. "I honestly don't know," I said. "They were just crazy rantings. Nobody threatened our lives or anything. Jenny may have kept them. I'll have to ask her Monday morning."

"Call her tomorrow and ask her," John directed firmly. "I want to get a look at them just as quickly as possible. Envelopes, too. The sooner we can get a handle on whether the writer is a man or woman, the faster we can get someone working on identifying him or her. If there's a connection, and the writer turns out to be this guy stalking Kate, we need to find him and question him before this thing escalates. From what you say, he sounds deranged. How dangerously, we can't assess until we talk to him."

"Or her," I reminded John. "We don't know yet that there's any connection between our penpal and my new shadow."

"Mmmmm. Point taken, but the odds are pretty good that they're one and the same person. We'll just have to see, but sooner would be better than later." He snapped his notebook shut and turned to Margo. "Doesn't seem to be anything more that can be done here. I'm going to make one more look around to make sure the house is secure, and then we can go." He rose and headed for the stairs to check out the upstairs one more time.

"Wow, and I thought my cautious Colombian was a security nut," I whispered to Margo. We collected the coffee mugs and headed for the kitchen. John bounded down the stairs and made a quick tour of the first floor, then joined us in the front hall.

"Are you coming with me?" he asked Margo.

"I can only hope," she said, and we watched him blush to the roots of his hair. "Is he cute, or what?" she said and patted his backside on the way out the door.

Six

On Sunday morning, I had trouble getting out of bed after my adventures of the previous evening, then decided to abandon the effort. Why not wallow in my last Sunday morning of single living, I reasoned as I leaned happily back against my pillows at ten o'clock with a mug of coffee and my address book. Microsoft Outlook was all well and good at the office, but it was hard to access from between the sheets unless you had I laptop. I didn't, so I settled in as comfortably as possible with Jasmine at my feet and Simon draped over my legs like fourteen pounds of road kill to make the phone calls I had promised to make this morning. But first, I called Armando.

"Wake-up call," I announced in response to his mumbled hello. "Time to get out of bed and enjoy your last day of unencumbered debauchery."

"Unencumbered whaa ...?" Some of the words I chose still confused him, since English was not his first language. "Oh." He chuckled to himself. "Just wait until next Sunday morning, and I will show you some debauch-whatever. So how are you doing this morning, *Cara*? What are your plans for this day, while I am safely out of the way toiling away at this packing, packing, packing. I cannot think how I am going to get it all done before the movers arrive tomorrow."

"I have a suggestion for you. Hire a dumpster, and heave ninety percent of that junk over the deck railing. You should have done it weeks ago." I had no sympathy for packrats, as he well knew. Saving his credit card statements was one thing, but saving the envelopes and the junk inserts that came with them?

Predictably, he changed the subject. "So how did you spend your Saturday evening without me?"

It was my turn to squirm. "Oh, girl stuff. Gave myself a pedicure and a facial, you know. We did have a little excitement, though." The trick was how to word this without getting him into a total swivet. "A man driving a van through The Birches was apparently knocking on doors, trying to get directions or something. One of my neighbors saw him knocking on my door, assumed he was a vandal and called the police. Can you believe it? Then they had to send a cruiser over, and I had to give a statement. It was all a lot of nonsense, of course, but I know you will agree that it is better to be on the safe side, right?" I swallowed hard, trying not to feel too guilty about my edited report.

There was a moment of silence. Then, "Why do I have the feeling that you are not telling me quite everything?"

"Oh, Armando, it was nothing, and the best part is, it's all over. Go have some coffee and call me later. I promise to be more sympathetic."

"And that you are in a big hurry to get rid of me."

"You're being very silly. I'll talk to you later. 'bye!" I finished brightly and disconnected. Quickly, I flipped through the pages in my address book to find Jenny's home number. Her mumbled "hello" brought me right back to my own misspent youth, when calling a friend before noon on a Sunday would have been unthinkable. I apologized for bothering her and asked if she had kept the strange mailings we had been receiving at the office. She was quiet for so long, I thought she had fallen back to sleep. "Jenny?" I prodded gently.

"Mmmm, yes, I heard you. I'm just trying to think. There were two of them, right? And the envelopes were hand printed in blue felt pen. Yes, I think I stuck them in the middle drawer of my desk. I was going to look up those crazy quotations on the Internet when I had a minute, but then I got busy and forgot about it. Why do you need them? Has something else happened?" She was sounding dangerously more alert every second. I had no interest in getting into an elaborate explanation of the previous day's events.

"Yes, but I can get them from you tomorrow morning. I just needed to know if you still had them. Don't give it another thought. See you tomorrow!" Once again, I disconnected hastily and moved on to my next call, but Emma's phone went right to voice mail. Officer Ron must still be on the premises, I reflected. "Hi, Em, me again. Kind of a flap here last night. Call me when you get a sec."

Before I got a chance to call her, Margo phoned me. "Well, hey, Sugar. You're sounding all bright-eyed and bushy tailed for this hour on a Sunday mornin', especially after all the excitement last night. What did that man of yours have to say about your adventure?"

"Some adventure! And if you think I gave him anything except the barest outline of what happened here last night, you're crazy. How about meeting me at the Town Line for a bodacious breakfast?"

No one would guess by looking at her svelte figure, but diner breakfasts were one of Margo's favorite things in the world, and the Town Line Diner in Rocky Hill served up her very favorite farmer's omelette. "You're on. See you there in half an hour."

Thrashing my way out from under Simon's bulk, I dashed for the shower and jumped into my weekend jeans and shirt. Make-up consisted of two swipes of mascara and one of lipstick. On my way through the bedroom, I yanked the sheets off my bed and dropped them into the washer in the hall. A little detergent and fabric softener, a few dial twists, and I headed for the door. As I opened it, I heard the phone start to ring. Instantly, I knew it was Armando, having rethought my sketchy account of the previous evening's activities and wanting to dig deeper. I slammed the door and ran down the garage steps to my car. Another five seconds, and I wouldn't have heard the phone ring, I rationalized.

Despite my speedy preparations, Margo managed to beat me to the Town Line. I pulled open the door from the big parking lot and took comfort from the familiar sounds and scents of the diner. Families fresh from church services occupied the many tables and booths, along with young couples who were probably still on last night's date and an assortment of regulars, of which I was now glad to be one. I was making my way to a booth at the end of the row by the front windows when Sherri, a regular Sunday morning waitress, pointed Margo out at the end of the long counter.

"So is this a bad omen?" I asked her over excellent coffee. "Sins of omission seem like a bad way to start off this new phase in our relationship." I had explained my heavily edited version of last night's visitor during my phone conversation with Armando this morning. Margo took a thoughtful sip of her own brew.

"Frankly, Sugar, I think that's a young person's perspective. Those of us with a few more miles on us have a different take on these things."

"Well, that's for sure, but what do mean in this case?" I prompted.

"When you're young, you believe with all of your heart that complete honesty is essential to a lastin' relationship ... with friends, men, whoever. Our parents drill that into us so we'll be truthful with them. But after dealin' with the fallout from all of that frankness and candor over the years, we learn that very often, complete honesty is not the way to go. If a friend asks you if she looks fat, and she does, you'd be crazy to tell her the truth. You make a huge mistake and cheat on your boyfriend with an old flame, and how does tellin' him about it improve things? You feel better because you've come clean, but he feels terrible. Much better just to mend your ways, keep your mouth shut and deal with your guilty conscience in silence. Then there are the social invitations you'd rather be shot dead than accept. A kindly fib is the only acceptable way out. You know what I mean."

Of course, I agreed with her. "But in this particular case, why am I hedging the facts with Armando?"

"Because you know Armando well enough to know that he'd get into a big, macho flap if you told him all the details, and what good would that do? The police are on the case. You and I are grown-up, sensible women and are on the alert. If you think about it, there's not a single thing Armando can do here to be useful, so why get him all riled up? It would be downright unkind, especially considerin' all of the stress he must already be under today tryin' to get ready for the big move tomorrow."

Just hearing her say the m-word made my stomach feel funny. "Speaking of stress ..." I stirred my coffee and chewed on a thumbnail.

"Oh, for heaven's sake, are you still obsessin' over this?" Margo slapped my thumb away from my mouth lightly. "It's perfectly natural to get cold feet at this stage, but we both know you're goin' to go through with it. In fact, if he called you right now and said he's lost his nerve and just can't move in after all, you'd be devastated."

I ran that scenario through my head and had to agree with her. I would be crushed. "So how do I get rid of these jitters?"

"You don't. You can't. You wouldn't be normal if you didn't have the willies after all these years of livin' by your lonesome. Havin' all that freedom and privacy was great, but Sugar, this will be great, too. Just put one foot in front of the other one for a few days, and the move will be behind you. You will have had your first spat or two, and kissed and made up, and it'll all turn out just fine. You wait and see. Now drink your coffee, and let's order us up an omelet and some home fries."

My butterflies flew away, and my stomach growled in anticipation. No doubt my misgivings would return, but for the moment, I felt undeniably better. I smiled at my friend and signaled to Sherri that we were ready to order.

"So what's the latest on the Henstock sisters' skeleton?" I asked after we had dithered happily for a few moments between bagels or croissants, English muffins or pumpernickel toast. "Any new developments from the good lieutenant?" At the mention of John Harkness, Margo's lips curved into a smile. If I didn't know her love-them-and-leave-them ways so well, I would be tempted to think she was besotted.

"Not much. The forensics report makes the remains those of a woman, youngish, Caucasian. No obvious signs that she was done in with a hammer or a bullet to the head, so cause of death is nearly impossible to identify. The fabric and the dye were aged at about sixty years, which means she went into that closet thingie in the basement around 1945, as near as anybody can say." She shrugged. "Weird to think that gruesome body was right in the house with them all that time. When did you say the Judge died?"

"The late 1960s, I think." I repeated what Ada and Lavinia had told me about their father's late-night visitors all those years ago. "Do you think the Judge knocked up one of his lady friends, then did her in and hid the body in the basement?"

Margo choked on her coffee and dabbed daintily at her lips with a naplin, wide-eyed. "Thank goodness there's so much chatterin' goin' on around us that nobody but me heard that. You are absolutely sick! Just because a mature, single gentleman feels the need of some, um, companionship from time to time and needs to be discreet because of his position doesn't make him a monster and a murderer!"

"All right, all right. It was just a thought. It's not that I begrudge the poor guy a girlfriend or two. It can't have been easy to be a single man in the public eye, having to raise two young daughters. But you have to agree, it's an interesting theory. Or maybe it wasn't murder at all. Maybe one of the ladies had designs on him, and when he rejected her and refused to marry her, she took an overdose and expired in his study just to make him suffer! And when he found her, he was afraid he'd be accused of murdering her, so he walled her up in the basement one dark night."

Margo stared at me. "Have you been watchin' daytime television? I cannot think how such a melodramatic solution to this little mystery even occurred to you ..."

Fortunately, Sherri chose this moment to deliver our breakfasts, and I was spared having to reply immediately. For a few moments, we busied ourselves with jam and butter, then forked into our omelets ravenously. I waited until Margo had her mouth full to forestall further comment from her. "This situation doesn't require any additional drama from me. I don't think even a soap opera writer could come up with this one. A woman's body is walled up in a local judge's basement for more than sixty years ... oh, no!" I dropped my fork with a clatter. "You don't think the poor thing was walled in *alive*, do you?"

For the second time in five minutes, Margo choked. "Who puts these ghastly ideas into your head? I had no idea you were so bloodthirsty. No, of course she wasn't alive. There was a family in that house, which is far from soundproof. And I don't care what they tell you in those trashy books you must be readin', a few bricks and some mortar are not goin' to silence somebody who's behind them screamin' her head off."

"Oh, thank goodness. Where was I? So the body is plastered up behind some bricks in the basement. The judge dies. The little girls turn into old ladies. Some pipes spring a leak, and they call a plumber. He goes down into the basement and rips out some bricks that are blocking access to the leaking pipes, and there's Skeleton Woman. He freaks and runs out of the house, never to return. The sisters call us, not the police, because they're afraid that having a corpse in their basement might be a turn-off to potential buyers for their house. By the way, do we actually have the listing for that yet? Then the police come, but the skeleton has disappeared, right along with the mystery plumber, whom nobody can seem to locate."

I chewed thoughtfully for a moment. Margo concentrated on her eggs in an effort to tune me out, but I continued. "Next, the body or remains or whatever turn up in the Spring Street Pond. Nobody has a clue about the identity. And oh, yes … coincidentally, I'm being stalked by a guy in a black van, but we don't know if that has any connection to the Henstock sisters' skeleton. How's *that* for melodrama?" I took a bite of my toast and waved at Sherri for more coffee, but before she could pour my refill, Margo put her hand over my cup.

"Thanks, Sugar, but I think this girl has had just about enough caffeine." Sherri laughed and departed while I pouted over my empty cup. Margo pushed my ice water a little closer. "Try some of that. I think you're overheatin'. Now, if we really must have this revoltin' conversation, at least let me finish my food first."

Twenty minutes later, sated with food and conversation, but having arrived at no plausible solutions, we inched our way through the crowd of diner patrons waiting in line at the register to be seated and pushed through the doors to the parking lot.

"What are your plans for the rest of the day?" I asked as we climbed the stairs to the second level and ambled toward our cars. "Are you and John doing anything this afternoon?" Margo arched an eyebrow. "Let me rephrase that. Are you and John doing anything *else* this afternoon?"

Margo giggled. "Why, I don't know just yet, but if we do, I'll tell you all about it tomorrow. How about you? Are you goin' over to help Armando finish packin'?"

"Nope, uh uh, no way," I said firmly. "Packrats have to pay the price for their hoarding. I know what's in that apartment. I've seen it many times. He has ten years worth of unnecessary papers, every book he's ever read, and clothes he hasn't worn since the 1980s. A lot of stuff is in piles on the floor. And I don't even want to talk about the kitchen. Our deal is that I get the house ready for him to move into, and he sorts out and packs his stuff. Anything that won't fit into his bedroom, bathroom and the loft area will have to be stored in the basement, neatly and in cartons. He's on his own with the packing." We arrived at my car. "I think I'll give Strutter a call and fill her in on last night. Maybe we can meet for coffee later. I'd love to get her to open up about what's going on with her lately."

"Make it a decaf," Margo advised. "I have a feelin' you're not goin' to do much sleepin' tonight as it is. You don't need to be loadin' up with caffeine on top of everythin' else." She fumbled in her stylish tote bag for her car key. "And Sugar?"

"Uh huh?"

"Watch out for strange men in black vans."

* * *

Late that afternoon, Strutter and I ambled along Old Main Street heading toward the Wethersfield Cove. Somewhat to my surprise, she had agreed to meet me for a before-dinner walk, although she had declined to stop for coffee along the way, citing the ubiquitous "stomach problems." As overstimulated as I already was, I was glad to take a pass on the caffeine anyway.

We spent a pleasant few minutes poking among the flats of vegetable and floral seedlings at Comstock, Ferre & Company, then crossed the road and headed downhill to the Cove. Basking in the warmth of the sun that had finally decided to acknowledge that it was summer, it was difficult to accept that we had passed the longest day of the year and were already losing a minute or two of daylight each day.

"What's with the stomach upsets? You seem to be having a lot of them lately. Are you feeling all right? Everything okay with John and Charlie?" I asked as we crossed the Cove's sandy parking lot and paused at the water's edge, causing my perceptive friend to cut her eyes sideways at me. My tone had been too casual, and she knew me too well. She stooped briefly to pick up a handful of pebbles and stood tossing them into the cove. A mirthless smile accentuated the turmoil in her eyes, which were the color of the Caribbean sea.

"You're right, of course. I'm pregnant. Six weeks gone, as near as I can figure. I was crazy to think you and Margo wouldn't pick up on it for a while yet." Plunk, plunk went the pebbles. I struggled to find the right words to say.

"But that's wonderful! Charlie must be so excited, and John ... well, he must be over the moon. What did he say when you told him the news?" I decided not to ask why she had not wanted Margo and me, her partners and best friends in the world, to know yet.

The pebbles were gone, but Strutter continued to stare at the horizon. Then she made her decision and turned to face me. "I haven't told John yet or Charlie, either. I don't know if I'm going to." She shrugged forlornly, and a tear straggled down her beautiful face.

"Don't know if you're going to ... here, let's sit down for a minute." I shoved her gently in the direction of a convenient bench and fumbled in my pocket for a tissue. "Now what's this all about? Spill it."

Strutter sat on the bench with uncharacteristic meekness and honked into the tissue. A quick glance around reassured me that we had the place practically to ourselves. The only other people in sight were a young couple walking their dog up toward the road. "I'm sure you're right about Charlie. He'd be out of his mind happy at the thought of a little brother or even a little sister." She paused. "It's John I'm not so sure about."

I ran a scenario through my head of her breaking the news to John Putnam and could imagine nothing but his handsome face wreathed in smiles. "But I know John was never married before, and he doesn't have any children. So this is his big chance! Every man wants a namesake."

"Maybe not. John's not a sweet young thing of thirty-seven like me, you know." She smiled bleakly. "He's fifty-one years old, Kate. In his mind, that's grampa territory, not an age when anyone wants to be up all night with a screaming baby."

I had to admit that I had never given the difference in age between Strutter and John a moment's thought. They had fallen for each other like a ton of bricks, and the joy they radiated obliterated any reservations they might have about something as unlikely as more children. The sobering reality of a possibly fractious infant shed a somewhat different light on the matter. "But surely you discussed this …"

"… before we got married?" Strutter finished my question for me. "Actually, we didn't. I know that seems odd, but, well, there was Charlie, and John was so taken by him, it seemed as if our little family was already in place. A son that age is just right for John, and Charlie followed him around like a puppy from the first time they met. John is the father he never had and always longed for. It was all perfect."

I cleared my throat, uncertain of how to phrase my next question. "But Strutter, unless you went into this marriage intending to be celibate—and the way you and John can't stand next to each other unless you're holding hands, I know *that's* not true—you had to acknowledge the possibility of conceiving a child. As you point out, you're still in your prime, Girl. Weren't you being ... careful?"

Again, the sad smile. "Sure, mostly. But once in a while, we'd get careless, and as I have good reason to know, once is apparently all is takes. Charlie spent the night with a friend back in the early part of May, and we opened a bottle of good wine, and ... well, here I am, knocked up like a teenager and just about as scared."

Concerned, I could understand. Upset was even within my ken. But scared? I turned in my seat and took her hands in my own. Despite the heat of the afternoon, they were icy cold. "Now what on earth do you have to be frightened about? Surely not John."

She squeezed my hands reassuringly. "No, no. You know that man doesn't have a mean bone in his body. John would be supportive, no matter what his feelings might be about this, which is why I haven't told him yet. No, it's not John I'm afraid of. It's me."

I squinted at her, struggling to understand. "You're being just a tad oblique here. I'm afraid you're going to have to spell it out for me."

Her eyes met mine fully for the first time. "I'm afraid that my carelessness about birth control is about to ruin the best thing that ever happened to me. I'm afraid of what this news will do to John's and my marriage and his beautiful relationship with my son. And maybe most of all, in order to prevent all of that happening, I'm afraid I'm going to have to have an abortion and carry the awful guilt of it to my grave." And at last, the long-repressed tears burst free in great, shaking sobs as I held her and patted her gently on the back.

As I waited for the storm to pass, I considered what she had confided to me. I could understand the cause of her distress. Whatever one's personal views happened to be about a woman's right to terminate an unwanted pregnancy, I knew that abortion remained a very personal issue. I also knew that for all of her loving tolerance of other people's choices, abortion had to be a last-ditch option for my Baptist-reared friend. Her back would really have to be against the wall for her even to consider it.

For all of her Jamaican gorgeousness, Strutter was not a tidy weeper. After five minutes of full-out blubbering, her sobs subsided, and she raised a reddened, blotchy face. My one tissue had long since passed the point of no return, so she had no choice but to wipe her streaming eyes and nose on the sleeve of her sweatshirt. "Don't tell anyone you saw me do this. Oh, god. Now I have a headache." She finished mopping her face and rolled up her sleeves to conceal the evidence of her inelegance.

"Mmmm. A good cry can be very therapeutic, but the headache is the price. A little better now?"

"I guess so." Briefly, she put her head down between her knees. "Increases the blood flow. Good for a headache," she explained in a muffled voice. After a minute she rolled back to an upright position. "Let's start back, okay?"

I nodded, and we got to our feet, heading slowly back through the parking lot to the street above. The air was noticeably cooler in the early evening, and it seemed as if all of Wethersfield had retreated to their homes and local restaurants for an early dinner.

"What should I do, Kate? I know it's not fair of me to ask you, but I need your advice. What would you do in my place?"

For a moment, I actually tried to put myself in Strutter's shoes. What would I do if I were faced with her dilemma? Then I realized the impossibility of trying to answer such a question, even hypothetically, and abandoned the effort. "I couldn't possibly know that unless it happened to me, and with the hot flashes I'm having, that's extremely unlikely. This sort of situation has way too many variables for me even to hazard a guess. There are the ages of the two people, how they feel about each other, where they are in their lives when it happens, who else is involved. But most importantly, I'm not you, and you're not me. There is no one, right answer, Sweetie. I will be thrilled if you and John decide to have this baby, and you all live happily ever after, but only you can decide if that's right for you and yours."

We trudged on in silence, Strutter massaging the back of her neck with one hand. "I know, I know. I just don't know how to do that."

"Maybe you're not giving John enough credit here," I pointed out cautiously. "After all, he's not some seventeen-year-old kid. He's a mature man, and maturity could work to your advantage here. He fathered that baby you're carrying. Don't you think he deserves some say in how this all turns out? You're in this together, and I think you're making a mistake by keeping it from him."

Nervously, I darted a glance at Strutter to see how she received this pronouncement, but she was too weary and headachy to take umbrage.

"I guess you could be right," she replied with uncharacteristic acquiescence. "Maybe I should tell him, I don't know. It's just that once I do, I can't take it back. It will be out there, shadowing everything else in our lives." She sighed heavily as we reached our cars. "I promise to give it some more thought tonight. By the way, what does Margo have to say about this? Oh, come on," she protested when I didn't answer right away. "I'm quite sure that Margo is well aware of my condition. She notices everything."

I admitted that Margo and I had both at least suspected that she was with child. "She was as tickled as I was initially. We just couldn't understand why you were keeping such wonderful news all to yourself, but we knew it was your decision to make." I stopped uncomfortably.

"Well, at least I've made that decision. Let's see how I do with the next one."

Seven

Margo had predicted accurately that I wouldn't get much sleep, but it wasn't caffeine or even agita about Armando moving in that kept me tossing and turning. I had pretty much made my peace with that for the moment. It would be what it would be, and I would deal with it as it happened. No, it was Strutter and her dilemma that was on my mind, followed closely by the man in the black van, and after that by the Henstock sisters' difficult situation.

Lavinia and Ada and Strutter and John all pinwheeled through my overactive brain until dawn, when, bleary eyed, I untangled myself from the sheets and plodded into the kitchen for some coffee. Jasmine appeared to beg for some tuna fish, and I was glad to be able to solve her problem, since I had no idea what to do about anyone else's.

Shortly before eight o'clock, I shut both cats into my bedroom with a litter box, water, and a bowl of crunchies. They were accustomed to this drill on days when I had outside workmen in to do the rugs or windows or one repair or another, and they accepted their fate fairly philosophically. The patch of sunshine on my bed was just as good for napping as the one in the living room, after all.

Before heading for the office, I dialed Armando's number. "How's it going?" I asked, determined to be cheerful. "All set for the movers?"

"They are already here, and no, I am not ready! I will talk to you later." Bang, down went the receiver. Not a good omen, I thought; but once again, I shrugged off my misgivings. Moving day was always awful. This one would pass, and then the worst would be over.

I let myself into the Law Barn, remembering my promise to get our anonymous letters to John Harkness today. The scene in the lobby as I approached Jenny's desk was pure *déjà vu.* Once again, Jenny sat holding a newspaper clipping in her hand. I said good morning and bent to read it over her shoulder. It was another story about the University of Connecticut's corpse flower, which apparently would reach its full and hideous glory sometime within the next week. A webcam had been installed so that anyone could tap into UConn's website and witness the foul-smelling flora at a safe distance, but those with less delicate sensibilities were lining up around the clock to visit the botany lab in person.

"So what's today's message for us poor sinners?" I asked Jenny when she turned the clipping sideways to read the blue block printing in its margin.

"'Not until it starts to stink does the inevitable happen,'" she read aloud, then turned to look at me. "I don't get it, do you?"

"Well, this one doesn't sound particularly Biblical, at any rate. Maybe our pen pal is branching out into secular sources. He or she does still seem hung up on this corpse flower, though, and the business about foul odors. Listen, don't touch this one too much." I held out a fresh zip-lock freezer bag that I had brought for the occasion. "Just drop it in here along with the envelope it came in. Did you find the first two, by the way?"

A worried frown settled on Jenny's pretty face. "Yes, they're here. What's this all about, Kate?" She pulled open her top drawer. Handling the previous letters by their corners, she added them to my pouch, and I slid it shut without touching them.

"I wish I knew." I gave her an edited version of Saturday night's attempted break-in, as I had for Armando, but law student Jenny was not to be fobbed off quite so easily.

"So the police are assuming that there's a connection between these letters and the intruder."

"Not assuming, exactly. They're just trying to get a handle on this guy, and these letters are a place to start. There may not be a connection at all," I told her.

"What about the situation at the Henstocks' house?" she persisted. "Could the fact that Strutter saw the skeleton have something to do with the attempted break-in?"

"I don't see how Strutter seeing the remains could result in someone following me. That doesn't make any sense to me."

"But you were there later. In fact, it was you who brought the police into it."

"Well, technically, it was Margo who called them, but yes, Strutter and I showed up with John Harkness in tow. If someone was watching the house ..." I trailed off, not wanting to dwell on that possibility. "Anyway, I'll get these over to the police department, and we'll see if they offer any clues. Is Strutter in yet?" I was anxious to see what her state of mind was this morning.

"No, but Margo came in about half an hour ago. She's in the office."

I gave Jenny a reassuring wink and went to collect a mug of coffee before heading down the half-stairway to the MACK Realty office. Despite the early hour, Margo was a picture of pulled-together perfection in a lime green linen capri pantsuit. She was curled up on the sofa, high-heeled taupe sandals standing neatly on the floor next to a matching tote. As usual, she was multi-tasking, talking earnestly to a client on the phone while her manicured fingers tapped busily at her laptop. She waggled a hand at me in greeting and brought her conversation to a close as I powered up my desktop computer and began checking emails.

"How did it go with Strutter yesterday? Did she fess up to being with child yet?"

"Yes, but there's more to it than that." I took advantage of Strutter's absence to fill Margo in on Strutter's dilemma while I zipped through my Outlook inbox, deleting junk mail as I went. I finished my recitation and looked up. I was surprised that Margo had made no comment, but when I saw her face, I grew truly alarmed. She stared unseeingly out the windows behind me, her face a frozen mask of distress. "Margo, what is it?"

She dragged her eyes back to my face. "Strutter's not serious about ... terminatin' her pregnancy," she said finally. Her face was chalky.

"I'm very much afraid that she may be," I reported. "She is clearly miserable at the prospect, but she seems to believe that an abortion may be the only way to salvage her relationship with John."

Margo sprang to her feet and paced the carpet without bothering to slip into her shoes. "But ... doin' that would most definitely ruin their relationship, doesn't she see? John would find out one way or another. These things are impossible to keep secret. And even if he agreed with her right to do it, he would look at her differently from that moment on. The damage would be irreparable. She has to tell him, let him help her make the decision, and let the chips fall where they may." She stopped pacing and demanded, "Where is she now?"

"I'm not sure. At home, I guess. Why?"

Margo reseated herself abruptly, thrust her feet into her sandals, then grabbed her tote bag and jumped back up. "Because she and I are going to have a conversation right now." Halfway up the stairs, she turned back. "Sorry, Sugar, but you're not invited this time. She needs to have this chat with someone who's been there and done that and can tell her what she would be lettin' herself in for." And she was gone.

I sat for a moment, allowing the full implication of her words to sink in. *Poor Margo, poor Strutter,* I thought. It's a choice no woman should have to make. Margo had never shared with me what had to have been a very personal and distressing experience, but it was clear that she was about to confide in Strutter. For all of Margo's exterior *bravada*, she was as tender as a marshmallow on the inside. I knew she could only be doing this in an attempt to spare Strutter pain that she herself had already experienced.

The ringing phone reminded me that it was time to get back to running our business, but I had one errand yet to do. I ran back up to the lobby and told Jenny to man the phones as best she could. I needed to get our hate mail into John Harkness' hands, and I wanted to see what, if anything, was new on the investigation of the Henstocks' skeleton. The thought of the impoverished old ladies sitting in that great house, worrying about their financial security, was more than I could bear.

On the drive to the Wethersfield Police Station, I allowed the idea I had had a couple of nights ago, but hadn't had time to explore, to resurface. I had seen only the first floor of the Henstock house, but that had been enough to reveal a once-elegant residence. The rooms were high ceilinged and delightfully proportioned. Windows and light were plentiful. Much of the woodwork and molding was still exquisite, not to mention the brass fittings on cupboards, closets, windows and exterior doors. A variety of hardwood flooring and still-gorgeous, albeit threadbare, Oriental carpets enhanced every room. The *porte cochere* and carriage house added exterior interest to a beautifully landscaped property, or at least, it would be beautiful if it got the attention it needed.

Needless to say, everything would benefit from a healthy infusion of cash to make necessary repairs and cosmetic improvements. If only it could house a business of some sort. Maybe it could be a catering establishment that could also host weddings and fundraising events. I had heard that there was a ballroom on the top floor and imagined a small orchestra playing waltz music while elegantly attired dancers circled the floor. The house had once been the *grande dame* of the neighborhood. She had fallen on hard times, but it was plain to me that the old girl still had good bones.

The irony of that observation under the present circumstances struck me funny, and I started to giggle — that is, until I glanced into my rearview mirror at a traffic light and saw a dark van with a tinted windshield close behind me. The laughter died in my throat, and I gripped the wheel tightly, hardly daring to breathe. I was on the Silas Deane Highway, just two long blocks from the police department. The light turned green, and with difficulty, I restrained myself from stamping on the gas pedal. Instead, I accelerated smoothly to a moderate rate of speed, and as the police department driveway came up on my right, I put my blinker on and turned in. Would the van follow? *No, of course not,* I chided myself. If this were the man in question, and I had no evidence that it was, this was not a destination to which he would follow me.

The van slid on by the driveway. I eased into the first available parking space and jumped out of the car. By craning my neck, I could just make out the rear of the van, which had been caught in heavy traffic at the next light. I couldn't read the license plate, but I was almost certain that the left rear taillight had only a partial cover. Or was I imagining that? I squinted into the morning sunlight, but a city bus blew by, totally obscuring my view.

I abandoned the effort and trudged into the police department. A young woman at the desk took my name and punched John Harkness' extension number into her phone. After a few murmured words, she hung up and reported that Lieutenant Harkness was unavailable at the moment, but Sergeant Fletcher could see me if I took the elevator up to the second floor.

As the elevator doors slid open, I was greeted by a beaming Rick Fletcher. I had always been fond of Rick. He had been in high school with Joey and Emma, and as a young officer with the WPD, he had helped me out of more than one tight spot. "Sergeant Fletcher, is it now?" I twitted him. "And when did this promotion take place? Not that I ever had any doubt that you would one day get the recognition you deserve."

"About a month ago, Ms. Lawrence, thanks. Come on down to my cubicle. The Lieutenant is out trying to track down that plumber who found the body at the Henstock house, but he said you would be coming by with some letters. Are these the ones?"

I handed over my freezer bag and took the chair next to his desk. "Yes, and we added another one to our collection this morning." I filled him in letter number three. "Today's quote didn't seem to be Biblical, but I'm not much of a student of the good book, so I can't be sure. I also have no idea if these letters and my would-be intruder are connected in any way. It's entirely possible that we're contending with two crazies here."

Reluctantly, I told him about the black van behind me on my way here. "But honestly, Rick," I concluded, I don't know if it was the same van. With one thing and another, I'm so on edge, I'll probably be seeing black vans around every corner for a few days. It seems as if every workman in New England drives one."

"Mmm." He looked up from his examination of the accusatory clippings, which he handled carefully with some sort of tweezer device he pulled from a desk drawer. "Well, it's a long shot, but we'll try to lift some fingerprints off these and run them through the system. I don't hold much hope, but we have to try. And without a plate on that van, we're pretty much dead in the water there. The broken taillight is purely anecdotal evidence, since that wouldn't be recorded anywhere." Noting my crestfallen expression, he quickly added, "But who knows? Maybe the Lieutenant will come up with the Henstocks' plumber, and he'll turn out to drive a black van with a broken taillight."

"… who used to be a priest and has an odor phobia," I chimed in. "Yes, that would be perfect, wouldn't it? Now if only he turns out to have a record, and his fingerprints are in the system!" Rick's phone started to ring, and I got to my feet. "Thanks, I'll keep in touch. No, no, I'll see myself out." I flashed him a smile and headed back to the elevator to face the rest of my day. As it turned out, it had only just begun.

* * *

Late that afternoon, the phone rang for what seemed like the hundredth time. Neither Margo nor Strutter had appeared, leaving Jenny and me to fend for ourselves. As much as I sympathized with Strutter's dilemma, I couldn't help feeling abandoned and resentful. I was having a bit of a day too, after all. My stomach had been in turmoil for hours as I contemplated what was happening at my formerly orderly abode and what I would have to face there this evening. Being left to hold the MACK Realty fort was the last straw. I snatched up the phone. "MACK Realty. Kate speaking."

"Oh, Kate, I'm so glad you're still there," blurted a voice that could only belong to Ada Henstock." I looked at my watch and saw that it was past four o'clock.

"Ada? Yes, the office is still open, although not for long. Actually, I had no idea that it was so late. No wonder I'm hungry. What can I do for you?"

Ada lowered her voice conspiratorially. "It's Lavinia. Frankly, I'm becoming quite concerned about her. All of this business about the skeleton in the basement, you know. She's become quite agitated, worrying about what's to become of us if we are unable to sell the house. I wonder ..." She paused.

I hastened to reassure her. "It's too early to assess possible interest in the property, since we can't list it until this mystery is resolved, but I'm certain that it's way too early to give up hope." I paused in my turn, then cleared my throat. Should I tell Ada my idea and risk raising her hopes falsely? "Actually, I've had an idea about the house. It's just a concept, and I haven't had time to think to think it through, but I would like to discuss it with you and your sister sometime. I know Strut ... er, Charlene has had the full tour of the property, but I would appreciate having an opportunity to see the upper floors, as well. It would be helpful if more than one of us were familiar with the entire layout of the house."

"I'm sure we would be very glad to see you whenever your schedule would permit. In fact," she rushed on, "if you're feeling a bit peckish, we'd be pleased to offer you tea this very afternoon. Nothing elaborate, but I do make a tasty cucumber sandwich, and Lavinia baked a batch of ginger snaps just this morning."

My stomach growled hungrily. I thought of the chaos awaiting me at home. Who knew when I would get dinner tonight? "I could come right now, if you like. Thank you for inviting me."

"Oh, my pleasure entirely," she assured me. "Do come right over. Lavinia will be so pleased to see you, as of course I will."

Half an hour later, replete with three cups of excellent Earl Grey tea and cucumber sandwiches, which were far tastier than I had anticipated, I followed Ada up a wide staircase across the main hall from the Henstocks' kitchen. "It's good of you to give me the grand tour," I offered as we climbed the curving steps at a decorous pace. Lavinia lingered in the kitchen to wash up.

"Oh, it's my pleasure," Ada assured me a bit breathlessly. She was well past eighty years of age, after all. "I don't often get the chance to show people around these days. Not that there's much to show any more," she concluded wistfully, glancing about her. Though tidy and obviously well dusted, the second story, when we reached it, had a sad, neglected air like a once-proud beauty when the bloom of youth had departed.

A second hallway, even wider and grander than the one on the first floor, spoke volumes about the wealth and status of the structure's original designer. Clearly, the Judge had had a taste for the finer things in life and the bank balance to procure them. Turning right off the landing, we made a complete circuit of the second story, opening doors into a series of bedroom-and-bathroom suites that must have constituted the height of elegance back in the day. Each suite offered some architectural detail—a marble-tiled fireplace, crown molding, or leaded windows framing a cozy windowseat—and boasted the wide-planked flooring and once dazzling Oriental carpets I had admired on the first floor. Throughout our round, Ada's hands trailed lovingly over this piece or that of what I was certain had to be valuable antique furniture, now piled willy nilly under dust covers.

"How charming! So inviting," I murmured as we moved from room to room, ending with the master bedroom suite. Ada confided that the massive four-poster that had once taken pride of place had been removed a few years ago. In its place stood two twin beds.

"We share this room now," Ada answered my unasked question. "Of course, we could each have a room of our own, but at our age, we prefer the company, frankly." I smiled to myself, wondering if Armando and I would ever reach an age at which we preferred to share sleeping quarters instead of having our own space. Thinking of Armando made me remember my promise to him that morning to prepare a home-cooked dinner for us that evening. Guiltily, I looked at my watch.

"Who used all of these lovely rooms?" I asked as we paused at the foot of yet another beautiful staircase leading to the third and top floor.

Ada smiled dreamily. "Guests," she replied, "lots and lots of guests. Nearly every weekend and all summer long the house was fairly bursting at the seams with houseguests. Mama was so beautiful and lively, and she adored fine music. And dancing! Oh, my, she loved to dance, and the Judge indulged her." Remembering her glamorous, young mother, Ada's eyes sparkled in her seamed face, and I could see the vestiges of the animated beauty Ada herself was reputed to have been in her own youth. "Let me show you something," she whispered. She held a cautionary finger to her withered lips, then pointed downstairs to where Lavinia lingered. "I haven't brought anyone up here in years. Lavinia finds it too upsetting."

Ada led the way to the third story, keeping to the outer edge of each stair to minimize the creaking. I did the same. At the top, we faced double doors of such ornateness, such beautiful craftsmanship, that I couldn't help but gasp, earning a disapproving shush from Ada. "Sorry," I whispered apologetically, "but even the hinges are works of art."

Ada's eyes shone at the compliment. "There's more, much more, but you must be as quiet as a mouse, or Sister will be up in arms." So saying, Ada produced a huge key from her apron pocket and used it to unlock the doors before us. She slipped the key back into her pocket and eased open the doors. She stepped into the room beyond, and I followed, heart thumping with excitement.

Despite the sunlight streaming through a half-dozen arched and recessed windows, it took a minute for my eyes to adjust to the relative gloom. Slowly, I understood that we were in the fabled ballroom, which ran the entire width and length of the third story. The sheer beauty of the room's graceful proportions took my breath away. I stood silently gazing around me, jaw agape.

Ada laughed softly. "It's quite something, isn't it? Oh, the parties Mama and the Judge held here, often until the wee hours of the morning. Sister and I were supposed to be asleep, but our bedrooms were just downstairs. We couldn't help but hear the music and the laughter, and, well, children will be children." She leaned closer and confided, "Sometimes, we would take our pillows and sit on the floor near one of the air shafts in Lavinia's room. We could hear everything quite clearly, you know." She gestured to the ironwork grill of a nearby opening to what must have been the same airshaft.

I smiled, imagining the two little girls in their braids and nightgowns, giggling in the dark at the sounds of the mysterious goings-on in the ballroom upstairs as their parents socialized with their privileged friends against the backdrop of live dance music.

A noise from downstairs startled us back to the present. Ada collected herself and shooed me back to the landing. She relocked the ballroom securely before we hastened down the stairs as quietly as we could manage it. Once safely back on the second floor, we grinned at each other in sheer pleasure.

"Thank you so much for sharing that with me, Ada. Tell me, why is the ballroom kept locked? It seems quite empty of valuables."

Ada shrugged. "Papa locked it after Mama passed, and I guess Sister and I have simply continued to honor his wish. After Mama's death, the joy just went out of this house," Ada explained sadly. "Papa loved her so. We were very young, of course, but we knew that. He never got over it, and I don't recall there being a single party of any kind here after that."

"Not even when you graduated from high school?"

Ada shook her head. "No, the Judge kept to himself, for the most part, and we soon stopped inviting our friends here. One by one, we just shut up the rooms, and after Papa died, well ..." her voice trailed off sadly.

Impulsively, I blurted out the idea that had been taking shape in my mind over the last couple of days. "Ada, have you and Lavinia ever considered reopening those rooms? Filling them up with guests and throwing parties again?"

Ada stared at me as if I had taken leave of my senses. "Having houseguests and throwing parties? My dear, even if we were so inclined, which it is difficult to imagine, in our present circumstances, we can barely afford essential repairs, let alone entertain a houseful of guests." She tsked to herself, obviously aghast at the thought of such frivolity.

"No, no, I haven't made myself clear." I collected my thoughts and began again. "What I meant to say was, have you ever considered opening the house up to *paying* guests, opening a bed and breakfast? Old Wethersfield attracts thousands and thousands of tourists every year, and with all of the other historical attractions and restaurants in this area, I'm sure people would stand in line to spend the night in an authentic French Second Empire house. And that ballroom! Just imagine a wedding reception with a small orchestra in the corner and round tables scattered around the perimeter with fresh flowers and people dancing ..." I stopped to assess the effect of my impetuous words on my companion.

Ada stood stock still, her eyes searching my face. *She's probably wondering whether to call her sister for help, since I've obviously lost my mind,* I thought, holding my breath. Then a slow smile curved across Ada's mouth and moved upward into her eyes. They glittered with an emotion I could not at first identify. Then I could. It was hope. "Do you think?" was all she could say at last.

"I do think," I replied confidently. "All it would take is someone who knows what they're doing and lots and lots of money."

As suddenly as it had appeared, the light faded from Ada's eyes. "But who would want to invest in a house where a body had been walled up in the basement?"

"You'd be surprised," I said wryly. My experiences of the last few years in the real estate business had opened my eyes to the public's thirst for gore. "In some buyers' eyes, a body or two in a house's history only adds a dash of drama, a little panache."

"Even if we never solve the mystery of how the body got there?"

"Especially if we don't," I reassured her sturdily. "People will happily supply their own explanations, however removed they may be from the facts." I'd had some experience in that area, as well. "Solving the mystery is only important in terms of closing the police file so that we can put the property on the market. For all I know, that might not even be required." I made a mental note to ask John or Rick about the legalities of the situation.

Ada apparently knew enough about human nature to recognize that what I said was true. She brightened immediately. "A bed and breakfast," she repeated softly to herself. "How Mama would enjoy knowing that." She grabbed my hand and tugged me toward the stairs. "Let's go tell Lavinia your idea right now. It could be just the thing to perk her up. She hasn't been at all herself lately."

* * *

However much I had tried to prepare myself for the invasion, the full impact of Armando's arrival in my territory still hit me like a kick to the solar plexus. I stood motionless in the kitchen and viewed the chaos of the center hallway, too shocked to speak or move. A dozen or more cartons blocked the doors to every below-counter cabinet, the oven, and the dishwasher. More were stacked slapdash against the front hall closet door, draped in a pile of coats and jackets. Instinctively, I set down my briefcase and went to hang them up the clothes before I realized that I couldn't possibly get the closet door open.

I went through the outerwear absently, recognizing most of the pieces from the years that Armando and I had been seeing each other. It was odd to see them stacked in my front hall awaiting a new closet. There were six windbreakers in varying weights and colors. Two raincoats, one long and black, and one brown and belted. Two winter-weight dress coats. Four sleeveless down vests, two with the TelCom logo on the left chest. The carton atop the stack contained piles of scarves, a dozen pairs of gloves, and assorted ear muffs and headbands.

The need for a medicinal glass of wine overcame my growing despair long enough for me to wrestle two cardboard boxes away from the cupboard that served as my liquor cabinet.   Carrying a glass of shiraz carefully, I picked my way through the debris into the living room. More cartons, two televisions, and several side tables of indeterminate function blocked the couch.   I changed direction and padded silently past the laundry closet and the powder room to my bedroom at the end of the hall. The door was closed, and for a moment, I couldn't think why.   Then I remembered Simon and Jasmine.   Poor kitties, presumably locked up in here all day.

I opened the door quietly and peeked in.   Blessed serenity met my gaze.   My neatly made bed with its coordinated floral-print pillow shams and dust ruffle looked as cozy as ever.   The colors echoed the brushed velvet upholstery of my sofa, faded with age but still elegant under the windows on the back wall. Among the plumped cushions lay my two old friends, who rose sleepily to greet me.   The used litter box and empty crunchies dish assured me their basic needs had been met, and I sank down on the sofa to stroke them.   For several minutes, I sipped my wine in the late afternoon sunshine and savored the orderliness of my familiar space.   A choppy purr emanated from first Jasmine, then Simon. The short hallway leading to my bathroom was flanked by closets.   It was blissfully free of clutter, and I knew that the bathroom beyond would be as tidy as I had left it that morning before leaving for work.

From the second floor, I heard muffled thuds and curses as Armando struggled with one piece of furniture or another.   *Let the adventure begin,* I observed wryly.   I thought of the long, upsetting day Armando must have had – was still having, I amended guiltily, and my heart at last went out to him. *This can't be easy for him either. At least I get to keep my address and phone number, as well as my bedroom sanctuary. He hates change as much as I do, and he's having to change just about everything.* Spotting the open door, the cats lumped off the sofa and went to investigate the interesting noises drifting down the hallway. I followed them back to the chaotic kitchen, where I poured a glass of wine for Armando and ordered a pizza. Then I climbed the stairs to see what I could do to help.

Eight

Despite the chaotic clutter that threatened to derail my civility, I took the first tentative steps toward establishing a daily route when I arose the next morning at my customary 5:30. I tiptoed into the kitchen, where I brewed a small pot of my half-caff coffee, fed Jasmine and Simon, and set out some frozen chicken breasts to thaw for dinner. Then I retraced my steps to my bedroom sanctuary, trailed by the beasts. We shared a blissful half-hour back under the covers while I planned my workday in my head. Returning to the kitchen, I poured my second mug of coffee, rinsed out the pot, and made a batch of Armando's special Gevalia brew while one of his favorite cranberry muffins from the Town Line Diner warmed in the microwave.

I readied myself for the office and tidied my bedroom. At 7:00, when I heard his clock radio click on to his favorite oldies station, I poured out his coffee and took it and the muffin upstairs to his room. Simon snored on the living room sofa, but Jasmine followed me curiously as I carried Armando's breakfast to him. He looked so vulnerable, curled up under his blue plaid bedspread, that I leaned over to give him a good morning kiss. My intentions were good, but the poor man almost suffered cardiac arrest when my lips touched his cheek and Jasmine simultaneously jumped onto his stomach.

"Whaa …!" he yelped, jolted out of somnolence. He propped himself up on his elbows and looked around himself wildly. When his brain processed the reality of his new surroundings, he managed a bleary smile.

"Sorry, Sweetie," I apologized. "How did you sleep?" I looked around for a place to put down the coffee mug and muffin. The surface of his bedside table was entirely covered by the clock radio, a lamp, a pile of magazines, his glasses, and what looked like a pile of mail. Determined to ignore it—his space, his rules, I perched carefully on the side of the bed, still holding his breakfast.

"As if someone had hit me with a sledgehammer. And you?" Noticing that my hands were full, he sat up and pushed things around on the bedside table until there was just barely room for me to deposit my burdens, then sank back against his pillows.

Jasmine, enchanted to find her favorite person in the whole world in her house at that hour of the morning, walked up Armando's chest, purring, and licked his ear. Armando grimaced and scooped her off his chest, where she settled down next to him. "Who invited you here? I don't want cat hair all over my bed." Despite his protestations, he reached out to stroke the old cat under her chin. She squeezed her eyes shut in bliss and raised the volume on her purr.

Armando's eyes drooped shut again, and I decided to make my exit. He didn't have to leave for his job at TelCom for a couple of hours, so why not let him sleep?

"Don't let your coffee get cold," I admonished, then gave up. I dropped another peck on his whiskery cheek and gave a thumbs-up to Jasmine, now curled within the protective curve of Armando's arm. I had faith in her ability to train him as completely as she had trained me in very short order.

Walking the circuit of the Broad Street green before work wasn't any fun at all without Emma, but with weeks still to go before her return, I knew I'd best get used to it. I completed my solitary lap at the Nathaniel Foote memorial monument, then headed toward the Spring Street Pond, where my car and camera awaited. I was well aware that Strutter was in crisis mode, and Emma was quite properly going about the business of living her own life, but it really was too bad of Margo to desert me during my domestic upheaval. Armando and I had survived our first night under a shared roof reasonably well, due mainly to our joint state of shock. Mutual exhaustion by ten o'clock had ensured a good night's sleep, which also helped. *One day at a time*, I told myself.

Still, I felt a little pouty as I scanned the reedy perimeter of the pond, Nikon at the ready. It was anybody's guess if the swan family would be in view this early, but I had promised Emma regular photo updates, so here I was.

A few geese caught the early sunshine on the bank nearby. A splotch of white caught my eye at the far side of the pond. I stood motionless for a full minute and was rewarded by the first viewing of the day of the swan flotilla. The proud cob led the way — or was it the pen? It was difficult to tell the male from the female unless they were in close proximity. Then his slightly larger size was evident. Anxiously, I counted the fuzzies paddling furiously in their parent's wake. I was fearful that the snapping turtles might have dispatched one or more of the young cygnets, since the duckling and gosling population seemed to have been seriously depleted during the past week. Two ... three ... four, and the remaining parent brought up the rear. I sighed with relief. I had heard from others that the swans made excellent parents, but until recently, I hadn't been sure why their young survived far more often than the other waterfowl. Then I had witnessed their dad in action.

One afternoon, as the swan family lolled in the sun on the grassy bank, a foolish goose had wandered over to investigate a crust of bread or some other detritus left by some well-meaning human who didn't realize how bad the stuff was for the birds. Intent on his trashy snack, the goose had come too close to the dozing cygnets. Papa swan, whose turn it had been to remain vigilant while his missus napped, sprang into action.

In two seconds, he was on his feet and had morphed into a monster swan, puffed out to twice his normal size. He had advanced on the luckless goose in full hiss, wings arched and neck stretched forward menacingly. The transformation stopped the goose cold. He backed off very, very slowly, his prize forgotten. When an appropriate distance had been re-established between the swan brood and the interloper, the cog offered a final hiss, then deflated and returned to preening his feathers as if nothing whatever had happened.

Now I smiled to myself, remembering the scene. Whatever the species, we parents were all alike. If someone or something threatened our babies, we were all capable of throwing an impressive hissy fit. I reminded myself that my baby was expecting an update photo of the swans and hurried to snap one to send to Emma later.

As I passed through the Law Barn's lobby a few minutes later, I was pleased to hear from Jenny that our disapproving correspondent had apparently decided to skip a day. That was a welcome surprise, as was the sight of Margo curled up in her usual spot on the sofa, checking e-mails on her laptop, as I entered the MACK Realty office.

"Well, hi there, Sugar!" She looked up from her task, the hated reading glasses on the end of her nose, and greeted me sunnily, but I was still miffed. "Are you and the Colombian feudin' yet, or are you still protected by cohabitation shock?"

I deposited my purse and coffee mug on my desk and busied myself changing from my walking shoes to office pumps. Hell would freeze over before I would ask about her dramatic exit of the previous morning or how her conversation with Strutter had gone. If they chose to keep secrets from me after all we had been through together, then so be it.

But Margo was no fool. Sensing the chill in the air, she promptly set aside her laptop and padded over in her stocking feet to wrap both arms around me where I sat. "Poor Kate," she murmured consolingly, "abandoned by her nearest and dearest friends on one of the most traumatic days of her adult life. I'm so sorry, Sugar." She released me long enough to spin my chair around to face her. "You know I'm just dyin' to hear all about it. Give." She wiggled her impeccably groomed eyebrows at me and crossed her eyes.

I thawed immediately, unable to resist Margo's silliness, and launched into a full account of the previous evening. Within minutes, we were laughing together about everything from the unbelievable clutter to Armando's naïve pronouncement about allowing no cat hair on his bed. Margo found that especially hilarious.

"Oh, that is too funny," she gasped, wiping her eyes. "I give Jasmine two weeks to have that man totally under her spell."

"One," I countered, and we were off in another gale of laughter. "Well, this has been very therapeutic," I sighed when I could speak again, "but now it's your turn. Anything you'd like to tell me?"

Margo's expression quickly turned pensive, but she met my eyes steadily. "Honey, you know I'd tell you absolutely anythin', but the fact is, you may not want to know this about me. It's not somethin' I'm proud of."

"You had an abortion at some point," I said, careful to keep my tone neutral. "I already figured that out." I gathered my thoughts and leaned forward to be sure I had her full attention. "Margo, do you have some twisted notion that I'm going to judge you for that? Any woman who came of age during the sexual revolution and *didn't* get pregnant was either plug ugly or damned lucky. I was lucky. Many of my friends weren't. Luck of the draw."

Margo's shoulders, which had been slightly hunched as if to ward off a blow, sagged with relief. "I should have known better. I *did* know better than to think you'd go all sanctimonious on me, but I'm still very glad to hear you say it." She dropped back onto the couch and began searching in her handbag for her compact, which she used to make some minor repairs to her eye make-up. Satisfied, she snapped it shut. "Strutter knows that, too. After all, she confided in you before me, remember."

I had to admit that was true. "So why all the secrecy?" I couldn't help but ask.

"Force of habit, I guess. You weren't raised in a particularly religious family, and your mama and daddy were nice, ordinary, middle-class people. It was easy for you to keep your adolescent escapades private, whatever they may have been. But for Strutter and me, it was different."

"What do you mean? Different how?"

Margo thought for a moment. "Strutter was the daughter of a Baptist minister. From the moment that baby girl could toddle, she was watched like a hawk by every self-righteous member of her daddy's congregation, just hopin' to catch her doin' somethin' embarrassin.'" She shrugged. "That's just human nature. You'd better believe that girl was married before Charlie was conceived." Charlie was Strutter's twelve-year-old son by her first husband, from whom she had long been divorced. "As for me, you know I was married to the mayor of Rome, Georgia's son in my impetuous youth. I've already told you about his skirt-chasin' ways and how I took my revenge by havin' affairs of my own, to my daddy's everlastin' disgust. What I haven't told you is that a much earlier fling resulted in a very unwanted pregnancy."

Margo's eyes went flat as she looked out the window and remembered. "I was nineteen, the summer between my freshman and sophomore years at Emory."

"You went to Emory University?" I couldn't keep the surprise out of my voice.

Margo shot me a look. "Are you saying that it's not possible to be gorgeous and brilliant, too? Hush, and let me get through this. I had a temporary job at the university bookstore. I had chosen to stay on campus for the summer to escape what I thought was my parents' excessive interest in my social life." She flashed me a grin that didn't travel to her eyes. "Probably a bad choice, now that I think about it.

"Anyway, into the bookstore one day walked Robert Branham. He was twenty-six, just discharged from the U.S. Army. He had been a paratrooper in the 82nd Airborne, all very excitin', and just about as good lookin' as it is possible for one man to be. I helped him find the textbooks for his summer classes, we got to talkin', and ..." She shrugged eloquently. "One thing led to another, and after a couple of weeks, nature took its course." Again, the bleak stare out the window. "I know you won't believe this, but Robert was my first."

"You first what? Oh!" I bristled at her assumption. "Why wouldn't I believe that? You've always had, shall we say, a healthy sexual appetite, but come on, Margo. I know you far too well to think you were ever a slut. We all had our youthful indiscretions, but I hope none of us is the naïve little fool she was at nineteen years of age."

Margo's mouth twisted wryly. "You've got a point there, Sugar. So there I was in mid-August, two months gone and scared witless. It did not even occur to me to tell my parents." She rolled her eyes at the idea. "Mama would simply have died from the shame of it, and Daddy ... well, things would just never have been the same between us. He had to be able to think of his darlin' daughter in a certain way, you know?"

I nodded slowly. I knew.

Margo gave herself a little shake and hurried on. "I won't bore you with the details, but you will recall that abortion was illegal at that time, so I couldn't go to a doctor. But Robert knew a registered nurse who helped girls like me out from time to time. She even let me stay at her apartment for a day or two afterward and supplied me with antibiotics to prevent an infection. Sally her name was. I remember that her cat had had a litter of kittens." Again, the sad smile. "It really wasn't at all horrific. Just sort of surreal, like it was happenin' to someone else entirely. I went back to work on Monday with no ill effects at all. Physically, that is."

I kept silent while she decided what else she wanted to say. "The thing is, what I needed to tell Strutter, is that there hasn't been a week since then that I haven't wondered if I did the right thing. It never goes away. In fact, my doubts get worse with each passin' year. Oh, I forgave that frightened nineteen-year-old who didn't think she had any other choice back then. But very soon after, and ever since, there's been this feeling in my heart." She pressed both hands to her breast and looked directly at me. "What if I hadn't done it, Kate? What if I'd tried harder to find another answer? I might have a big, strappin' son with his daddy's good looks or a gorgeous, grown-up daughter with my amazin' style and charm." She made a self-deprecating face. "Wouldn't that be somethin'?" she finished sadly.

I lost my struggle to keep my emotions at bay, and my eyes filled with tears. "But Margo, things were so different then. The social mores were determined by how our parents had been raised, and back then, an out-of-wedlock pregnancy would have shamed you and your family. You didn't think you had a choice because you really *didn't* have a choice, or not one that you could live with. Today, you would have a dozen options and would feel free to choose among them. But back then, you would have done anything in your power to avoid hurting your parents. I understand that completely."

I stood up to give Margo a hug, but she waved me off lightly. "No, no, we'll have none of that. I've already repaired my face once this mornin'. I just thought Strutter needed to hear what I just told you from someone who's been through it before she rushes off to some clinic. And now you've heard it, too."

She looked at her watch and leaped to her feet, scrambling as always to locate her discarded shoes. "I've got to get over to Vista Views again. I'm fillin' in for Strutter today, but she'll be along tomorrow. Rhett's out back in the pen, so ask Jenny to keep an ear tuned, okay? You know how those squirrels love to taunt him. And Kate ..." She stopped and gave me a rueful half-smile. "Don't agonize for me, or for that matter, for Strutter. I've lived with my mistakes for a lot of years now, and I'll go right on livin' with them. Strutter has more choices than she thinks she has. She just needed that pointed out to her. She'll be just fine, I know it."

And for the second morning in a row, Margo ran up the stairs to the lobby and was gone, leaving me with one hell of a lot to think about.

* * *

The rest of the day passed uneventfully. In fact, the phone barely rang, giving me the entire afternoon to catch up on paperwork and send the morning's swan photo to Emma via e-mail. Rain clouds darkened the sky in mid-afternoon, and I switched on my desk lamp to brighten the office. Looking up the half-stairway to the lobby, I saw that Jenny had done the same thing.

The cool rain continued to fall as I made my way home to The Birches that evening. It had become my habit to check my rearview mirror frequently for black vans, but the rain and the headlights in the early dusk made it impossible to pick out colors. I arrived at the condo without incident and activated the electric garage door opener with the programmed button on the Altima's visor. Once again, I was grateful for the attached garage that sheltered me and the groceries I had bought on the way.

Armando had left work early to spend a couple of hours minimizing the remaining clutter on the first floor. By the time I let myself into the kitchen, I was pleased to see that the cartons that blocked cabinet doors had disappeared along with those that had been stacked in the hallway. I felt cheerful enough to call out, "Lucy, I'm ho-ome," in my best Desi Arnaz imitation as I set the green tote bag loaded with the makings of a spaghetti dinner on the table and went to hang my raincoat in the front hall closet, which was surprisingly tidy.

"Very funny." Armando leaned over the loft railing and blew me a kiss. "How was your day, *Cara*?"

"Why don't you come down here, and I'll tell you all about it?" I invited, smiling up at him. For perhaps the thousandth time in the five years I had known him, I was enchanted by his Latin good looks.

As I concocted pasta sauce and Armando assembled a big salad, I filled him on my tour of the Henstock house and my idea about turning it into a bed-and-breakfast. Throughout my recitation, he listened closely, as he always did when I spoke to him. Although his concentration was probably due partly to the fact that English was not his first language, I still found his attention charming and warmed to my story.

"That beautiful old house is really something. You wouldn't believe how lovely some of the rooms are despite years of neglect. That wide, planked flooring and recessed windows, some of them with windowseats. Straight out of a Jane Austen novel. And the marble-tiled fireplaces in the bedrooms, most of them still functional. Even the proportions of the rooms are appealing. And that ballroom on the third floor! I can just see a small wedding or a fundraising event, maybe a wine tasting. If that kitchen were updated, it could cater all sorts of parties, Armando. The possibilities are endless, and it's right on the Broad Street Green, which gives it all sorts of historical appeal. It shouldn't be too difficult to attract an interested investor, do you think?"

"It is a very interesting idea, but as the older Miss Henstock mentioned, there is the problem of the skeleton. What is happening in that regard?"

I repeated my theory that the mystery of the skeleton in the Henstocks' basement would only heighten the public's interest in the property.

"The public, yes. The public always has an avid interest in such things, does it not? But potential investors might well be reluctant to put money into what amounts to a crime scene. What progress has been made in the investigation?"

We moved into the living room, where I opened the glass doors to the fireplace and put a match to the wood fire I kept laid in the grate, ready for an evening like this. The dry wood caught quickly, and bright flames quickly sprang to life. As if by magic, both cats materialized and settled onto the hearth rug. A fire in the fireplace was a top draw, second only to dinner being served.

"According to Margo, who gets her information from John Harkness, of course, the police have been unable to identify the body. As far as the medical examiner can determine, death occurred in the mid-1940s, and the body was walled up very soon thereafter. Notices have been published asking for information surrounding the disappearance of a forty-ish woman around that time, but so far, no one has come forward."

I pulled the firescreen shut and adjusted the glass doors for maximum draw. "They've also drawn a blank on the plumber who found the body. The card he gave Ada turned out to be bogus. The phone number on it is no longer in service, and the company name on the account was fictional. John says they may never be able to close this case."

I sank down onto the sofa next to Armando, whose arm automatically lifted to make room for me next to him. *This is nice,* I thought contentedly as the aroma of marinara mingled pleasantly with a whiff of wood smoke. *I could get used to this.*

Armando was silent for several minutes, gazing at the fire. I hoped he was having similar thoughts about our new domestic arrangement. "So what do you think?" I finally prompted him.

"About what?"

"About the Henstock house. What do you think about finding an investor and converting it into an elegant bed-and-breakfast?"

With the fingers of his free hand, Armando gently tipped my face up to his. I felt the full voltage of his warm brown eyes as they smiled into mine.

"I think we should get married," he said.

Nine

As if my universe were not already reeling, our censorious correspondent was back the next morning with his most alarming message yet. "What makes you assume it's a man?" Jenny asked, holding the unopened envelope by one corner. "Couldn't a woman be capable of a stunt like this?"

She had a point. I had good reason to know that a woman could indeed be our poison pen-pal. A couple of years back, a local businesswoman had been similarly tormented by a female blackmailer. She had turned out to be a religious zealot, or "nicey-nice behaving badly," as Margo put it.

Using the letter opener Jenny handed me, I carefully slit open the envelope, again postmarked Storrs, Connecticut, and shook out a single piece of white paper and a news clipping. Holding the paper open at one corner, I poked it open with the letter opener and read aloud: "The dogs shall eat Jezebel by the rampart of Jezreel." I looked at Jenny blankly. "Yikes."
"On second thought, maybe you're right. A woman might pull another woman's hair out, but throwing her to the dogs is definitely a guy thing. But which one of us is he so mad at?"

"I don't know, Jen, but I'm starting to take this a whole lot more seriously." I thought for a minute. "Maybe if we found out what Jezebel did?" I suggested.

"Good idea." A true child of the information age, Jenny quickly Googled the name Jezebel, reviewed the first page of hits, and selected a Wikipedia entry. " 'Jezebel is introduced in the Bible as a Phoenician princess, the daughter of the King of Sidon, who marries King Ahab. She turns Ahab away from the God of the Jews and toward the worship of the Phoenician god Baal. Furthermore, she uses her control over Ahab to lead the Hebrews into idolatry and sexual immorality.'" Jenny scanned the rest of the article quickly. "There's a lot of fury and smiting and battles, as you would expect, but here's what we want. Some guy named Jehu is finally appointed by the god of the Jews to kill Jezebel. It says, 'Jehu then confronts Jezebel in Jezreel and urges her eunuchs to kill her by throwing her out a window. They comply, tossing her out the window and leaving her in the street to be eaten by dogs. Only Jezebel's skull, feet, and hands remained.' Nice, huh?"

"Lovely," I agreed, but my attention had been captured by the final words of the Wikipedia account. "Only Jezebel's skull, feet, and hands remained," I repeated. "Remind you of anything?"

"Oh, wow! The skeleton in the Henstock house. That clinches it. These letters are definitely connected to the body in their basement."

I remembered the newspaper clipping. "I suppose this is more about that smelly corpse flower." I nudged it around on the desk so we could both read it.

Corpse Flower Ready to Bloom, *June 23, 3:05 p.m. US/Eastern. Storrs, Conn. (AP)* Wait until the neighbors get a whiff of this. A giant exotic plant that has not bloomed in the Northeast in more than 60 years is ready to flower at the University of Connecticut's greenhouses.

The "corpse flower has the odor of three-day-old road kill, and UConn botanists couldn't be more excited. Once open, the spiked, bright red bloom even resembles rotting meat, a veritable welcome mat for the insects that pollinate it — flies and carrion beetles.

"It looks like something has died. It smells like something has died. It has some of the same chemicals that dead bodies produce," a UConn research assistant said today.

The plant is expected to blossom in the next five to six days. Already at 4 feet high, the flower could reach more than 6 feet high and at least that wide when it opens up. The stinky botanical curiosity is expected to attract visitors like ... well, flies. It will last just two days, and UConn plans to extend visiting hours at the research greenhouse to accommodate the nosy. A Web cam on the UConn Internet site provides odorless footage of the flower.

"Huh," I said, perplexed. For the umpteenth time this week, I felt a prickle of fear. "All I know is that something about this corpse flower has our friend all whooped up. It seems connected in his warped brain to whatever transgression he believes one of us has committed — or something that poor woman in the Henstocks' basement did. Maybe it's both, I don't know, but unless I miss my guess, he's also linking the time this thing achieves its full glory to when he plans to punish us." I plucked a tissue from the box on Jenny's desk and used it to scoop the envelope and its contents into a manilla folder. "That means we had all better be especially careful over the next few days. I'll take these to the Police Department this morning. Maybe this time they'll be able to lift some prints off the letter."

I retreated to the Mack office and sat brooding over a mug of coffee as I considered the events of the previous evening. Interestingly, I found the prospect of being eaten by dogs only slightly more alarming that that of entering into a second marriage. I loved Armando with all my heart and was completely committed to our relationship for the long term, but my views on voluntary *versus* legal commitment had not changed since I shared them with Margo. I had been shocked to discover yesterday that apparently, Armando's had.

"Think about it, *Mia*," he had persisted over glasses of port as the last of the fire hissed in the grate. "The children will be happy. It is time. I don't want to be, how do you call it, roommates. I want to be married to you."

Idiotically, my mind had latched onto his reference to Emma and Joey. *Some children,* I scoffed inwardly. Emma was twenty-eight, and Joey had reached thirty last November. Both had active, adult lives of their own ... so much so that Emma was a hundred miles away, and I hadn't heard from Joey in more than a week. Where was he anyway? I dropped my aching head into my hands.

Too many mysteries, I decided. *Do what you can with the information you have.* I dug two Advils out of my purse and washed them down with coffee.

While the ibuprofen worked its magic, I punched on my computer and began to respond to inquiries about one or another of Mack's property listings. Margo came in at nine, the ever-faithful Rhett at her heels, and joined me on phone duty. Just as I was about to ask if she had heard from Strutter, the Jamaican beauty herself strolled down the stairs. She had never looked better, and she walked her old walk into the office as if she had never been absent. She struck a pose, hands on hips, and waited.

Mercifully, the phones stayed silent, since Strutter was obviously bursting with news. "What?" we said simultaneously. I held my breath, and I had a feeling that Margo did, too.

A huge grin split Strutter's face from ear to ear. "I told John I was pregnant, that's what. Furthermore, I told him I had decided to have the baby, and if he didn't like it, he would be forcing me to choose between him and the baby, and he really didn't want to go there." She paused for dramatic effect.

Margo and I exchanged dumbfounded looks. "And?" I prompted obediently.

"He looked at me as if I had totally taken leave of my senses. Then he called me a whole string of names I can't remember, except they all seemed to be synonyms for world's biggest fool. And then he said, 'Let's go tell Charlie he's about to have a little brother or sister to boss around.'" She did a little wiggle and a hip bump. "That man is not just happy about this, he's thrilled. I don't know who acted like the bigger kid last night, him or Charlie, but both my guys are officially over the moon, and now I can be, too. I can never thank you enough," she finished, looking from one to the other of us. "You are the best friends I ever had."

That did it. The room exploded into celebratory hugs and laughter, causing Jenny to come to the top of the stairs to ask what all the excitement was about. We told her, tripping over each other's words, and she screamed and clapped both hands to her head. After another round of hugs, she said, "This is the best news ever. I just thought you'd figured out who our unwelcome correspondent is."

Questioning looks from Strutter and Margo prompted me to share the latest missive with my partners, and our mood quickly sobered. "I don't like the sound of this one," Strutter offered. "Up until now, the letters have been the usual crackpot ramblings of some self-righteous fool, although there was always something about that stink blossom ..."

"Corpse flower," I corrected automatically.

"Ooooh, that name," Margo shivered. "Can you imagine how hideous? And people are just linin' up to be disgusted by it."

"Mmmmm, just like rubberneckers at the scene of a car accident," I agreed. "I can't understand it myself, but there's some two-day-old roadkill on Prospect that's getting pretty ripe. Maybe we can sell tickets, a buck a whiff."

Strutter made a face and clutched her stomach. "Please! My stomach is touchy enough."

"He said something about a Web cam, or at least the newspaper did," Jenny remembered. "Let's take a look."

Before we could get on line, my cell phone rang, and I glanced at the display. Probably a wrong number. Most of my friends know better than to call my cell phone during the workday. Then I recognized the phone number of my long-lost son. "Sorry. I've got to take this," I apologized and took my phone closer to the back windows to get a better signal. "Joey!" I answered as my colleagues trooped up the stairs to investigate the UConn Web cam site on Jenny's computer. "I was beginning to think you were a figment of my imagination and Emma was really an only child."

"Yeah, yeah. I'm sorry, Ma. I've just been really busy."

"So I understand. What's her name?"

Obviously, I had taken him by surprise. "What's whose name? Oh!" He laughed sheepishly, and imagined him squirming, just as he had at the age of twelve when I'd caught him on the phone with his first girlfriend. "Justine," he said finally. Might as well get it over with.

"Tell me."

"She's the night manager at a grocery store on my Monday-Wednesday-Friday route. We'd talk whenever I ran into her on the loading dock. It was part of her job to check in deliveries," he added in explanation. "Anyway, we just hit it off, and I asked her out."

"Uh huh. More, please."

He took an extra beat, then sucked in a big breath and blurted, "We've been seeing each other exclusively for more than a month now, and the lease was up on her apartment, and Armando was moving in with you anyway, so I needed to find a place of my own for the nights I'm off. That's why

I'm calling, to give you my new address." He paused again. "And to tell you that Justine's my new roommate."

I was a trifle taken aback, but not shocked. Actually, I was secretly tickled that my nomadic son was sufficiently smitten to have a serious lady friend. He was well over twenty-one, and presumably, so was Justine. I put him out of his misery.

"Think we could meet her before the wedding?" I twitted him, then instantly regretted it. Who was I to be joking about roommates and weddings at this interesting moment in my life?

"I'll try to arrange it," he responded in his old smart-aleck fashion, clearly relieved to have the Telling of the News behind him. So what's new with you?

I told him, leaving out the more alarming parts. Why was it that I could never seem to trust the men in my life with such information? Part of it was that I had been cursed with an independent streak. Another part was my deeply held beliefs about the nature of women versus the nature of men. My daughter and my women friends could be concerned about me and help me out from time to time without smothering me with over-protectiveness. Men just had to step in and take over as if I were a complete idiot. It was beyond annoying. Besides, I really believe men enjoy an opportunity to kick a little butt. It's the nature of the beast.

"Call your sister," was my parting shot to Joey before I disconnected, although it was probably unnecessary. He and Emma had scrapped their way through childhood, always at odds, but maturity had brought them close together. That was as it should be. Well, at least one of my mysteries had been solved, and her name was Justine.

By late morning, things had pretty much returned to normal at Mack Realty. After spending a few minutes ogling the ghastly corpse flower on UConn's Web cam, as well as the dozens of eager spectators queued up to see it, we marveled at the public's insatiable appetite for the grotesque. This corpse flower thing had all the trappings of a freak show, but in this case, the freak was botanical.

"How would you like to be that poor guard who has to stand next to that smelly thing all day and monitor the crowd?" I pointed out a burly black man standing to one side of the exhibit. Occasionally, he would step forward and move whoever was at the head of the line along. Two minutes seemed to be the limit, according to the clock that ticked along at the upper right of the screen. I couldn't imagine wanting to be in that hideous flora's presence for even one minute. The Web cam image was enough for me.

Nestled in its huge, hothouse pot, the three-foot-wide *titan arum* was a sickly green. The open blossom, if you could call it that, was nearly black. Protruding obscenely was the spadex, a cylindrical column of the same, sickly green as the blossom. It extended fully four feet into the air and had Margo and Jenny giggling at the obvious parallels to male genitalia. Only Strutter remained silent.

"That's not a guard. That's just a lab employee. See the UConn identification badge on his shirt pocket?" She leaned closer to the screen for a few seconds, frowning. An odd expression came over her face.

"Feeling okay?" I asked.

"Yes, I'm fine. It's just that there's something familiar …" she turned back to the screen and pointed to the guard. At that moment, the website switched to another camera, and the guard was blocked by a spectator.

Margo looked at her watch. "Time to get movin,' ladies." We were all shocked to discover how much of the morning had evaporated and quickly dispersed to our various duties. Strutter took off to open the rental office at Vista View. Margo had an eleven-thirty appointment to show a house over on Garden Street. Knowing she would be glad to have an excuse to stop in and see John, I handed her the manilla folder containing today's hate mail to deliver to him. Jenny busied herself at the copier assembling more information packets on Vista View, since we were running low. I retreated to the Mack office to man the phones.

Shortly after one o'clock, my stomach reminded me that I hadn't eaten since dinner last night, and I volunteered to get a pizza from the diner at the corner of Church Street for Jenny and me. I welcomed the opportunity to stretch my legs on such a beautiful afternoon and strolled happily down Old Main Street. Abby Dalton, the owner of the diner, was a good friend, and it would be good to say hello and catch up.

Old Wethersfield was busy as local workers flocked to the diner and the boutique eateries that lined the street. Whether your tastes ran to homemade soup, fresh croissants, pizza or old standards like burgers and fries, you were sure to find it here.

In the two years since Mack Realty had taken up residence in the Law Barn, we had become acquainted with most of the business owners, and I was greeted with many waves and smiles as they bustled back to their shops and offices after squeezing quick lunches into their busy days.

Now that I was watchful for vans, it seemed to me that every other vehicle parked along Old Main Street was a beat-up work van. Lots of them even had broken headlights or taillights. Presumably, their owners didn't bother to repair them because they were driven primarily during the day. A blue one parked in front of Wethersfield Travel caught my eye. Festooned with ladders, pails and ropes, with magnetic signs proclaiming that it was the property of Best Painters affixed to both sides, it was typical of the battered vehicles favored by local service people, except that this one was in pretty good shape. A fresh coat of paint covered most of the dings and dents in the old workhorse.

I mused that they must have become their own customers. A shiny black one a few spaces further down gave me pause until I saw the logo of a Hartford office supplies store that routinely made deliveries in this area. The young driver lounged in the front seat, one foot propped on the dashboard, cell phone to one ear. Were young people never at a loss for conversation? Perhaps because I spent so much of my work day on the phone, I kept my cell phone for emergency use only and usually had it switched off. Because of recent events, I had taken to keeping it with me and switched on. Occasionally, I even remembered to recharge the battery. I patted it in my pocket now and went inside the diner to say hello to Abby and collect my pizza.

Late in the afternoon, long after Jenny and I had polished off a large part of the sausage-and-mushroom special, I was surprised to get a call from Lavinia Henstock.

"I'm so sorry to trouble you, Kate, but I wonder if I could possibly impose on you to drop by the house again this evening."

That was the longest sentence Lavinia had ever uttered to me directly, and I was immediately concerned. "Is everything okay, Lavinia? Did you hear something from the police department?"

"Fine, fine," she replied absently. "In fact, Sister and I have been told that we can go ahead and have the plumbing repairs completed in the basement. We've had a locksmith in to change the locks on all of the exterior doors, of course. Just a precaution, you know." She cleared her throat. "Ada mentioned your idea of turning this house into a bed and breakfast as an alternative to selling it."

"How do you feel about that?" I prompted.

"Oh, fine, fine," she repeated vaguely. Clearly, that wasn't the topic uppermost on her mind, but she couldn't seem to get to whatever did hold the top spot. I waited as patiently as I could, picturing the old dear standing in her kitchen, perhaps fidgeting with the telephone cord or the strings on her ever-present apron. "Ada will be out for the evening. It's her monthly bingo night at the church." Another pause.

A thought occurred to me. "Are you uneasy about being in the house alone, Lavinia?" How terrible it must be to be afraid of being alone in the house she had grown up in, but under the present circumstances, I could understand it. The saddest part was that I was the only one the poor darling could think to call to keep her company. It underlined how much the old ladies had come to depend on each other. But Lavinia surprised me.

"Goodness, no," she protested with vigor. "Nothing like that, nothing at all." After a final hesitation, she plunged into the real reason for having reached out to me. "Our recent, uh, unpleasantness has jogged my memory, you see. I've remembered something. At least, I believe I've remembered something. At my age, it's sometimes difficult to tell if one is actually remembering a real incident or if one's mind has created a fiction, rather like a dream, based on a snippet of long-ago conversation. In any event, I believe Ada might find this upsetting. I'm quite old enough to know that very often, it's best to let sleeping dogs lie, so before I contact that nice Lieutenant Harkness ..." I could almost see Lavinia patting her hair into place. "... or risk unnerving Ada, I wonder if you would be willing to hear me out and give me your considered opinion."

Quickly, I reviewed my evening agenda: Close up the office, feed the cats, and reheat the pizza left over from lunch for my solitary dinner, since Armando had a business thing to endure at TelCom. "Would seven o'clock suit you?" I offered and was gratified by the relief in Lavinia's voice.

"Admirably, thank you. Perhaps you would enjoy a glass of sherry. It's one of dear Papa's after-dinner customs that Sister and I have continued."

I assured Lavinia that a glass of sherry would be most welcome and ended the call, my curiosity thoroughly aroused. After clearing up a few odds and ends and shutting down my computer, I made short work of closing up the office and headed for The Birches. I strolled out to collect my junk mail and bills from the mailbox at the end of my driveway and met my neighbor Mary Feeney, who had come out to do the same. "I only collect this stuff once a week. There's never anything interesting any more. Any repercussions after the attempted break-in?" she asked idly, sorting through the appalling stack of wasted paper in her gnarled hands.

For the sake of keeping a lid on neighborhood gossip, I minimized my misgivings. "I wouldn't even go so far as characterizing it as an attempted break-in," I laughed it off. "Probably just someone lost who saw my light on and rattled the doorknob when I didn't answer the bell."

"Uh huh. And then he went around and rattled the back doorknob for good measure." Mary glanced at me shrewdly through her Coke-bottle lenses. "I always do that when I'm lost in a strange neighborhood. Calling the police gives the locals something to do on a Saturday night."

"Okay, okay, it was an attempted break-in. I think. Oh, I don't know, but whatever it was, it's over. And now that Armando has moved in, you don't need to worry about me any longer."

"How's that going?" she asked, cooperating in my effort to change the subject, and we spent another couple of minutes laughing about my adjustment pains before returning to our respective units.

After I fed Jasmine and Simon, and shared one bite of sausage each with them from my reheated pizza, I left a brief note for Armando on the counter next to the stove. He always switched the heat on under the kettle first thing when he entered the house so he could make himself a cup of tea. "Keeping Lavinia Henstock company for a little while," I wrote. "Home by 9:00. XO" As I anchored the note under one of the floral mugs from the cupboard, I chafed a bit at having to report my whereabouts. At the same time, I enjoyed knowing someone might actually give a rap about where I was. The conflicting emotions annoyed me, as always, and I shrugged them off. What was my problem? It wasn't as if Armando would restrict me any more than it would occur to me to restrict him. I felt certain I could leave him a note saying, "Having dinner with George Clooney. Back when I'm back," and upon my return, he would merely grin and ask if I'd had fun. Checking in with the person who shared your home was just common courtesy. Would marriage change that?

The evening was still warm, so I tossed a light jacket over my arm as insurance against the chill that would come later and picked up my purse. Instead of debating the merits of marriage, I'd do better to focus on Lavinia and whatever she was about to confide to me.

10

Shortly after seven o'clock, I was ensconced in the Henstocks' front parlor with a glass of excellent sherry in one hand. A gentle breeze wafted in from an open window overlooking the porch. "The kitchen is cozy for tea or coffee," Lavinia opined, "but Papa always thought that sherry should be served in the parlor. She patted a fat, terrier-sized dog of mixed heritage that was squeezed in next to her in her wingchair. Henry by name, he was a recent addition to the Henstock household and had set up quite a ruckus when I appeared at the kitchen entrance. "Arf-arf-arf-arf-arf!" he yapped shrilly now, jangling my nerves for the second time since my arrival.

"Henry, do be quiet," Lavinia admonished ineffectually. The smith who had changed the locks had apparently persuaded the ladies that a watchdog would be the most effective deterrent to unwanted visitors. To their credit, they had adopted Henry from a local rescue group, but I was somewhat mystified by their selection. My idea of a watchdog would be a shepherd or a doberman; but what Henry lacked in size, he made up for in volume.

I attempted to find a more comfortable position on the tufted settee. Henry and I regarded each other warily. No doubt he gave the sisters some much-needed companionship, and if his raucous greeting upon my arrival was any indication, I doubted that future visitors, invited or not, would go unannounced. "I'm sure the Judge was right. This sherry is absolutely delicious, by the way." I took another fortifying sip, moving slowly and unthreateningly under Henry's beady gaze.

"Thank you so much for agreeing to see me, my dear. And how is Mrs. Putnam?" Lavinia was having trouble getting around to the reason she had asked me to visit.

I smiled at her formal reference to Strutter. "She's very well, as a matter of fact. She and her husband learned recently that they are expecting a child in December. It might even be a Christmas baby."

If I had worried about offending Lavinia's delicate sensibilities with this news, I needn't have. "I just knew it!" She beamed with delight. "There was something about her the last time she was here ... a radiance, you might say."

"I'll be sure to give her your regards. Now Lavinia, I confess that I'm very curious to know what you've remembered, or think you've remembered, that might shed some light on the, um, remains found in your basement." I sat back carefully, mindful of Henry.

"Yes, of course. I'll get right to it, but first, let me refill your glass." I was astonished to discover that my stemmed crystal glass was already empty. As I said, it was exceptionally good sherry.

Lavinia refilled my glass and topped off her own, then squeezed back into the wing chair, where Henry had appropriated more than his fair share of space. "There's a good doggie," she praised him, presumably for allowing her to share her own chair, which she did by easing him over to one side. "Now, let's see. You may recall that when you and Lieutenant Harkness were having tea in our kitchen the other day, I mentioned that some years after our mother passed on, the Judge sometimes ... entertained a lady friend in his office during the evening."

I nodded encouragingly. "Yes. I remember Ada seemed very surprised to hear that. As I remember it, Ada was a bit more social than you were as a young woman, and she was often out with her friends while you stayed here in the house. Naturally, you would have a better idea about the Judge's habits."

Lavinia smiled and patted Henry's head while I sipped more sherry. To my eye, the dog looked quite smug. "Delicately put, my dear. But do you recall that I mentioned one evening in particular? It was around nine o'clock, I think. Ada was out, and I went downstairs to make some tea for myself before retiring with a new novel. I could hear voices coming from Papa's study, one of them a woman's. On impulse, and partly out of curiosity, I confess, I tapped on his door to ask if he and his visitor would like some tea. I was surprised when he didn't answer, and when I tried to turn the knob to poke my head in, I was even more surprised to find the door locked from the inside. I went straight to bed, and neither Papa nor I ever spoke of the incident again."

I imagined trying to get up the nerve to bring up a subject like that with my own father, shuddered, and took another sip. "I can certainly understand that."

Lavinia gazed through the windows behind me, becoming lost in the memory of that long-ago evening. "What I didn't tell you or Ada or the good lieutenant was that I remembered something else about that night. I heard two voices in Papa's study, a man's and a woman's. But it wasn't just conversation going on in there, oh no. Just as I approached the study door, the woman became quite distraught, almost hysterical, you might say. I couldn't hear most of it, but there was something about her husband knowing, or having found out something, and then what sounded like crying. Quite naturally, I believe, my instinct was to help her, even if my father was in there with her. I tapped on the door and tried the knob. The voices stopped but not before I heard distinct shushing noises. I realize now that Papa must have been trying to get her to quiet down." She paused. "Since I didn't hear her make another sound, he must have succeeded."

I refrained from commenting, not wanting to break her reverie, and swallowed the last of my sherry. Her revelations were disturbing, to say the least. Slowly, her eyes left the window and refocused on mine. "Do you see? I never heard her make another sound." And then Lavinia, too, fell abruptly silent.

We sat like that for a moment, considering the implications of what the young Lavinia had heard. Henry, growing bored with human conversation, scrambled to the floor and trotted off busily to the kitchen. I thought back to what Lavinia had told us earlier. "If I remember what you said correctly, it was right after that when the Judge arranged to have the special closet built in the basement."

"Why, yes, it was. Something about diaries and trial records that he wanted to keep for his memoirs but he didn't want anyone else to see. I thought it was other people's secrets he was trying to keep, but now ... now I'm not so sure. For one thing, why would he have anyone else's diary? That's a very personal record, not a legal document."

I gave that some thought, and I had to admit it didn't make any sense. I took a deep breath and came right out with the question on the tip of my tongue. "Lavinia, do you think your father was having an affair with a married woman, and that was the secret he wanted to keep?"

Her eyes grew round with distress, but she answered me unwaveringly. "That has occurred to me. It was wartime. Most of the younger men were serving, and many had been gone for years. Papa was a very distinguished-looking man and very popular with the ladies. It's not entirely unthinkable that ... well, that he became inappropriately involved with one of his clients." Further than that, Lavinia could not bring herself to go, and I didn't push her.

As gently as I could, I asked, "But even if that were true, and I'm not saying it was, why on earth would he want to keep any sort of documents in the house that might point to such a relationship?" Then I answered my own question silently. *Blackmail. Either he was blackmailing the woman, or more likely, he was using the papers as insurance against her blackmailing him.*

If that possibility had occurred to Lavinia, she didn't mention it. "I have no idea whatever. I don't like to keep secrets from my sister, but I truly don't see what useful purpose it would serve for me to confide all of this to Ada. It was a very long time ago, and her memories of dear Papa are precious to her." She took a breath. "What I need to know is, should I tell any of this to the police? Might it help solve this dreadful crime?"

It was a poser, for sure. On the one hand, Lavinia's recollections might well help trace the identity of the body. Surely, there must be records of women reported missing around that time. The flip side was that Lavinia's memory of the evening in question might not be accurate. It had been more than sixty years since she had overheard the scene in her father's study—or thought she had. She herself had questioned the accuracy of her recollection. I struggled to think of something wise to say, but in the end, I had to promise to give it some hard thought and telephone her before lunch tomorrow. This called for consultation with Margo and Strutter.

"Arf-arf-arf-arf-arf!" This time, both of us were startled enough to jump. We had been so focused on our conversation, we hadn't noticed that dusk had fallen outside the parlor windows; and while Henry could certainly be heard, he was nowhere in sight.

"Goodness! It's nearly dark outside. Let me turn on a lamp. Where could that silly dog have gotten to?" Lavinia got to her feet rather unsteadily, whether from the effects of the sherry or from sitting too long, it was hard to say. She groped her way to a side table and switched on a lamp, then looked around for Henry. "Henry! Come here! There's a good dog." She clapped her hands together sharply and waited expectantly.

The evening breeze coming in the front window had turned sharply cool, and I shivered slightly. "Do you mind if I close this window?"

"Not at all," she responded distractedly and moved into the hallway leading to the kitchen. "Henry! Where have you gotten to?"

I rose to my feet and realized that the sherry had been a lot more potent than I thought; but then, I had consumed a good deal of it, thanks to Lavinia's hospitality and Henry's yapping. So much for sherry being the genteel libation of clergymen and old ladies. This stuff packed a wallop. With difficulty, I wrestled the window shut and tottered after Lavinia. Halfway down the hall, the basement door stood open. "Arf-arf-arf-arf-arf!" shrilled Henry from the nether regions, and my heart sank. No amount of sherry in the world was going to make me happy about going down into that basement again, but I could hardly let an eighty-something-year-old woman tackle those stairs, not to mention that dog, on her own.

Nevertheless, that seemed to be precisely what Lavinia intended to do. "Now how did that door get open?" she mused, twisting the doorknob. "I'm quite certain the locksmith tested this new lock before he left." She pushed in the button that locked the door from the hall side. Then she shut the door firmly and twisted the door again. "See? It works perfectly. Oh! Ada must have left the door open when she came up with the sherry from the wine cupboard." She tsk-ed her annoyance. "Now Henry has got down there." Recklessly, she yanked the door back open and started down the dark stairs, feeling for the light switch.

Horrified at the possible consequences, I moved to help, if not stop, her. "I'll get the light," I offered, but despite repeated flips of the switch, the dim bulb I remembered hanging from a cord at the foot of the stairs refused to light. Perfect. Muffled growls and yips attested to the fact that Henry was indeed in the basement. If I really had to go down there after him, I wanted some light. "Wait, Lavinia. Let's get a flashlight, at least." I groped down two more steps unwillingly, feeling my way along the wall, but Lavinia had already reached the bottom of the staircase.

"Henry! Come here at once," she commanded sharply. To my utter amazement, he obeyed, flying past us up the stairs and zooming down the hallway, giddy with his adventure. Lavinia, who was obviously familiar with the basement terrain, reappeared from the gloom and climbed up to join me. "Well, that's a relief," she remarked, and I heartily agreed. Henry scampered back down the hall to the kitchen, where he became unusually quiet. Having a drink of water, perhaps.

I had reached the top step, with Lavinia right behind me, when the door slammed shut. Clunking and rustling sounds emanated from the other side. Had Henry bumped the door shut? "Oh, dear," said Lavinia, clutching my shoulder. Oh, dear, indeed. I felt for the door and tried the knob. Securely locked, of course, thanks to the shiny new hardware.

"Now what?" I asked a bit sourly. This evening was going downhill fast.

Lavinia sank to a sitting position on the step below me. "Now we wait for Ada to get home from bingo, I suppose. I can't think of anything else to do, can you?"

If I had my cell phone in my pocket, where Emma and Margo were always telling me to keep it, I could have called someone for help. But I didn't. It was upstairs in my purse, which I had set down next to me in the parlor. My heart rose as I heard distant sounds from somewhere in the house – the kitchen? the parlor? – followed by footsteps. Thank goodness. It had to be Ada, home early from bingo. "Hello!" I called out loudly to attract her attention. "It's Kate and Lavinia. We're locked in the basement." I pressed my ear to the door to get some idea of Ada's whereabouts.

"Arf-arf-arf-arf-arf!" yapped Henry gleefully a few inches from my ear, and I fell backward over Lavinia, tumbling down and down the dark staircase until the blackness in my head became one with the darkness that engulfed us.

* * *

The first thing I saw when I opened my eyes was Armando's face scrunched into a worried frown. "Hi, Handsome," I greeted him idiotically, then winced as the pain from the back of my head, right elbow, and left ankle hit me in that order. If I had expected tender expressions of concern from the love of my life, I was disappointed.

"*¡Nunca creí que fueras tan supremamente estúpida!*" He rose from where he had been kneeling next to the parlor settee on which I lay and stalked to the doorway leading to the hallway. He folded both arms across his chest and scowled as two paramedics, apparently called during my black-out, attended to business. When they had finished shining flashlights into my eyes, fitting me with an air cast, and wrapping my elbow in icy packs, they took their leave, admonishing me to go straight to the nearest emergency room if I experienced double vision or nausea. The younger of the two, himself a Latino, gave Armando a calculating look in passing. "*Cálmate, hombre.* Chill." Fat chance.

"Oh, dear," Lavinia fluttered as Ada showed the two men out. "Is he upset?" She glanced nervously at Armando, who maintained his rigid stance in the doorway.

"That would be my guess," I agreed. I had reason to know that under stress, Armando reverted to his native Spanish. I hadn't understood every word of tonight's commentary, but the part about my being incredibly stupid had come through loud and clear.

"Perhaps I shouldn't have called him, but he was the emergency contact person listed on the card in your wallet. I'm so sorry to have had to look through your things," Lavinia apologized yet again.

I struggled to a sitting position. Henry jumped up on the settee next to me and lapped wetly at my face, a conciliatory gesture after his part in the evening's drama. Since he was still festooned with cobwebs from his basement foray, and his breath was redolent of whatever his evening snack had been, I wasn't particularly happy about this improvement in our relationship. However, one look at Armando, glowering darkly at me from across the room, caused me to rethink my alliances. Any friend in a storm.

When we arrived home, Armando installed me in my bedroom with absolute correctness, comforter up to my chin, herbal tea and Advil on the nightstand. Throughout the short ride home, which we had made in his sporty little Honda, leaving my car to be collected in the morning, our conversation was perfunctory. Could I manage the low seat? I could. Did it need to be adjusted to accommodate the cast on my leg? No, it was fine.

Having done his duty as a gentleman to his satisfaction, he bid me a cool goodnight, no kiss, and withdrew haughtily to his bachelor quarters on the second floor. Well, at least the events of the evening had served to shelve any further discussion of marriage. I knew Armando well enough to know that the root cause of his anger was his fear that something terrible might have happened to me. I could only imagine his feelings as he tore through the night after Lavinia's call announcing that I was unconscious following a serious fall down a flight of stairs, and the paramedics were in attendance. Once his fear had been assuaged, he allowed himself the luxury of being furious at my putting myself in such a precarious position. Apparently, going down into a dark basement to retrieve a ditsy dog was man's work. Had I called him, or presumably some other man, to take care of the matter, this whole situation could have been avoided, his thinking would go.

I also knew that he was capable of maintaining his chilly reserve for days. He was a sulker. I tended to flare and cool in rapid succession, but Armando could nurse the coals of his anger for quite a while. Frankly, it was one of his less attractive traits. When we had lived apart, it was easy enough to tolerate his pouting. I just went about my business and waited for the thaw. Living under the same roof made things more difficult. Too difficult? I wondered.

A glance at the clock on my night table confirmed that it was only quarter past ten o'clock, the shank of the evening for those under thirty, so I did what I often did when I felt abused and abandoned. I picked up the telephone and punched the speed dial code for Emma. Within moments, I had the comfort I needed, with Emma laughing so hard that she had to go find a tissue for her streaming eyes. She knew Armando well, too.

"I can just picture you going ass over teakettle down those stairs and Armando's face when he heard you'd gotten yourself locked in that creepy cellar," she gasped. Then, more soberly, "I'm sorry you're banged up and hurting, but Momma ..."

I waited for her to express concern that I might well have broken a hip, but no.

"… you might have killed poor old Lavinia!" And she was off in more gales of laughter.

"Thanks for your concern," I said when she came up for air, "but poor old Lavinia is a lot tougher than she looks. It's that dog who was in danger of my murdering him."

"How on earth did he manage to shut the door anyway? You said he's not very big."

I gave it a moment's thought. "I'm not sure. He was so excited about his basement adventure, he was running around like crazy. I actually thought he had gone into the kitchen for a drink of water, because he seemed to quiet down, but then the door slammed shut. I mean, it had to be Henry. There was no one else in the house. Or maybe a breeze from the open window in the parlor blew down the hall and caught the door just right."

I stopped as two unwelcome memories surfaced. The first was my wrestling the parlor window shut just before Lavinia and I had headed for the basement. The second was the image of the kitchen door standing open to the evening breeze when I had arrived at the Henstock house. I decided to keep silent until I could consider the implications with a clearer head.

"Anyway, bad luck, Momma. So what else is new?"

Our conversation wandered into the more familiar territory of speculation about Joey's budding relationship with Justine and Emma's chafing under the never-ending surveillance of Officer Ron. Like mother like daughter, I supposed, amazed yet again at the characteristics that seemed transmittable via the gene pool. On that disquieting thought, our conversation ended, and I slipped into as deep a sleep as my aches and pains would allow.

11

As always happens with fall injuries, I awoke before dawn the next morning hurting in places I hadn't even known I had before my fall. Not only were my head, elbow and ankle throbbing as excruciatingly as expected, but new twinges in my hip and back had joined the chorus of pain. I groped for the bottle of ibuprofen next to the bed and washed down three tablets with a mouthful of cold tea, then lay still to await whatever relief they might provide.

By some miracle, I fell back to sleep, or perhaps I passed out. Whatever the cause, the respite was welcome, as was the mug of hot, strong coffee Armando brought me at seven-thirty.

"Thank you, thank you," I gushed gratefully, struggling to sit up. He set down the mug, grabbed me under both arms, and hauled me to a sitting position, none too gently. "Thanks again," I said dryly as he pushed pillows into place behind me and handed me my coffee.

I had expected him to stalk coldly from the room after performing these duties, but he surprised me by sitting down next to me on the bed. "Now," he said, "perhaps you will be good enough to let me know what the hell has been going on."

Before last night, I might have been tempted to go on with my little white lies of omission, as I thought of them, but one look at Armando's face made me give it all up. No, he would not understand why I hadn't told him about the man in the van and the fright he had given me the weekend before Armando moved in. Yes, he would obsess over my once again being embroiled in some sort of intrigue involving a religious lunatic who had apparently taken issue with something that Margo, Strutter or I had done that offended him. And possibly, he would not forgive me for not telling him about everything that had occurred over the last week. Armando was Armando. We didn't think the same way about everything, and I didn't always love what he did, but I loved him, and he loved me. If we were to make a life together, such secrets would not do. It was time to tell it all and let the chips fall where they may. So, I did.

Once I got started, I couldn't stop. The words poured out of me as I unloaded all of my frustration about being the possible target of yet another unbalanced stranger with a thing for a flower that smelled like roadkill, my fears about Van Man, who might or might not be stalking me, and my angst over the Henstock ladies and what would become of them if we couldn't solve this mystery and sell their house for them.

After a while, Armando held up a hand and took my coffee mug back to the kitchen. He returned with a refill and a mug for himself and resumed his seat at the side of the bed, but by the time I finally ran down, he had moved to the other side of the bed and lay next to me, his head cushioned with the sham-covered pillows that matched my floral bedspread. He lay quietly with his half-empty mug of cold coffee on his chest, and the expression on his face was inscrutable. *Probably wondering how quickly he can get the movers back here,* I guessed miserably, but he actually looked more thoughtful than angry.

"So?" I couldn't help but prompt him. Best to get the fireworks about my various deceptions over with.

He cut his eyes sideways at me and handed me his mug, which I deposited alongside mine on the bedside table. He rolled onto his side to face me and propped his head on his fist. I turned gingerly to face him, wincing as both ankle and elbow protested this movement. To my astonishment, Armando's eyes glittered not with anger but with amusement. "So it appears that I am living with Miss Nancy Drew, or how do you call her, the busybody who lives in Cabot Cove, Maine, and finds bodies wherever she goes?"

The comparisons rankled a bit, but I opted not to push my luck. "Jessica Fletcher, who writes mystery novels and must be well into her sixties. And I am not a busybody."

"I see. In your case, the mysteries come to you, not the other way around."

"Well, yes." *Mostly.*

"Then it must be part of your cosmic destiny to solve these puzzles, is it not? And I must do what I can to help you," he added, knocking me completely for a loop. Just when you think you know someone.

I stared at him. "Who are you, and what have you done with Armando?"

He lay next to me in his Mickey Mouse tee-shirt and plaid boxer shorts, his customary sleeping attire. His hair was a mess, and he hadn't yet shaved. In my eyes, he had never looked sexier, and I heartily regretted the injuries that prevented my acting on that thought. Eyes still twinkling, he replied, "I know you very well. You are stubborn and independent, and you will do what you will do. Whatever that is, I will be on your side." He pulled me close to him and whispered into my ear. "But *Cara*, if you ever conceal from me such a thing as an intruder who may wish to do you harm, I will lock you in a closet and push your meals under the door for a month." So saying, he reached around me and administered a sharp whack to my backside.

"Hey!"I protested, but secretly, I was somewhat relieved at this return to normalcy. For a while there, I was afraid he had undergone some sort of personality transplant. "Deal," I agreed, smiling into his eyes.

Abruptly, he released me and bounded to his feet. "Now what?" I asked with some alarm.

"Now I'm going to stick your head in the sink."

"Is that some sort of kinky punishment thing like locking me in a closet?"

He smiled broadly. "An appealing thought, but no. I am going to help you wash your hair. There seem to be cobwebs in it."

* * *

"Few things make a girl feel more attractive than having black toes." Armando had finally gone to work, but only after double-checking the locks on every door and window in the house. We had decided that more than my hair needed washing, so he had helped me in and out of the shower, then into a soft sweatsuit that pulled easily over my battered elbow and ankle. For the moment, I was without the aircast on my ankle, since I had it packed in icebags for the prescribed twenty minutes. It was too warm for socks, so I was stuck looking at my grossly discolored foot. To pass the time and distract myself from the throbbing pain, I was on the phone with Margo, filling her in on the events of the preceding evening.

"Sounds lovely, but it probably serves you right." I was beginning to resent the distinct lack of compassion I was receiving from my friends and loved ones. "With the secrets you've been keepin' from your man, you're lucky you don't have two black eyes to match 'em." I had also told her about my morning confessional.

"Is that some sort of ethnic slur? Because I have it on good authority that only eighty percent of Latino men beat their women," I said, voice dripping with sarcasm.

"Lucky you to have one of the others. But gettin' back to the matter of last night, why didn't you call me?"

"Because I was unconscious." I could picture Margo rolling her eyes, but she refused to rise to my bait.

"If your phone had been in your pocket, instead of in your purse ..."

I had heard that litany one too many times. "So where's your cell phone?"

"What do you mean, where's my cell phone? I'm talkin' on it! How big a bump is on that head of yours anyway?"

Damn. "You know I meant where do you keep your cell phone, generally speaking?"

There was a pause during which Margo decided whether to lie like a rug or tell the truth. Since she knew I was perfectly aware where she kept her cell phone, she opted for the latter. "In my purse, as you well know ... but when I leave my purse behind, it goes right into my pocket. What good is an emergency phone if it isn't with you in an emergency, I'd like to know?"

"Okay, okay, you win, but I wasn't expecting an emergency," I finished lamely.

"Nobody ever does, Sugar. That's exactly my point." Wisely, she changed the subject. "Are you absolutely certain it was that yappy little dog that pushed the cellar door shut? I can't imagine my darlin' Rhett doin' such a silly thing."

I had to admit that I was not at all certain, and since I myself had closed the parlor window before the door incident, the theory about the breeze having caught it didn't really work either. I mentioned the kitchen door through which Lavinia had admitted me, then left open to the evening air while we drank too much sherry in the parlor. Margo got quiet, and I could hear the unpleasant alternatives bouncing around in her beautiful head.

"So after goin' to all the trouble and expense of havin' the locks changed, Lavinia just left one of the most easily accessible doors on the first floor wide open, is that it?" I admitted that it was, but in her defense, she wasn't alone in the house. I had been with her the whole time, as had Henry.

"Judging from the commotion he raised when I came to that door, I can't imagine that he would have been any less alert to another, uh, visitor. He would have barked his head off, just as he did when I arrived."

"Tell me again exactly what happened after you and Lavinia started down those dark stairs. Oooh," she shuddered delicately. "The thought gives me the creeps."

I closed my eyes and concentrated, trying to get the sequence of events just right. "Well, Lavinia went down first. I was at the top, flipping the switch, but the light wouldn't go on."

"And you're sure Henry was actually in the basement at that time?"

"Yes, because we could hear him. And before I even got down the stairs, Lavinia called to him. I remember, because I was shocked when he actually obeyed her and zoomed up the stairs past me."

"Then where did he go?"

I thought for a few seconds. "I heard him run into the kitchen. I thought he must be having a drink of water, because he got quiet for a while. I don't remember what he did after that."

"So you and Lavinia climbed back up the stairs, but before you got to the top, the door slammed shut."

"Yes."

"And you saw nothin'? Heard nothin'?"

I squeezed my eyes shut harder. Then I remembered something else. "I actually did hear something, some rustling or clinking, coming from the other side of the door. I thought it must be Henry's tags. And then I heard what I thought were footsteps farther away from the door, and I knew Ada must have gotten home early from playing bingo at the church. I called out to her, and ... well, you know the rest of the story."

Again, Margo was quiet. "How quickly did Ada open the door?" she asked finally.

I had to admit I didn't know, having knocked myself out when I fell backwards over Lavinia.

"I'm not sure. I mean, Lavinia had to be groping her way back down the stairs to see what had happened to me, and Ada might not have heard me the first time I called out. I guess it could have been a few minutes.

"So you can't be sure the footsteps you heard were Ada's at all?"

I really didn't like the sound of that, but I had to concede the point. "Are you saying that someone else came into the house while Lavinia and I were in the cellar and deliberately locked us down there? But why? And how did he get past Henry?"

"I don't think he did get past Henry, at least not in the direction you're thinkin'. I think he came into the house right after you did, while Henry was still preoccupied with you and Lavinia in the parlor. I think he was in the house the whole time you were, and when you and the dog were in the basement, he saw his chance to sneak out. Henry didn't come when Lavinia called him. He heard someone walkin' around upstairs and ran upstairs to investigate."

"But he didn't bark," I protested weakly, appalled at the scenario Margo was creating.

"Because the intruder was ready with some hamburger or steak or somethin' else that dog just couldn't resist, and as soon as Henry's mouth was full, he shoved that cellar door shut and walked out through the kitchen, same way he came in earlier."

As much as I resisted this line of reasoning, the facts seemed to support it more than the assumption that a fifteen-pound dog, new to the household, had figured out how to close a heavy door and done it for no reason at all. I remembered Henry's wet kisses and the smell of something on his doggie breath. "But why?" I squeaked unhappily now. "If he meant us harm, he had us right where he wanted us. Why would he just leave?"

Margo chewed on that for a while. "Because it wasn't you or Lavinia he was after. It was something that he believes is in that house, something he didn't get the first time he visited."

"Do you mean the plumber?"

"Yes, the mysterious plumber, but unless I'm very much mistaken, he's not really a plumber at all."

My head started whirling again, and I leaned back against the sofa carefully. "What are you saying? Do you think the man at the Henstocks' house was the guy who's been following me in the van? Or is the guy in the van our poison pen-pal?" *Or do three entirely unconnected men have it in for me for some reason?* No, that was simply too paranoid to express even to Margo.

"I don't know what I mean, Sugar. This is all terribly confusin', but I need to call John and tell him about this. I'm sure he'll want to speak to you later."

I was sure he would, too. I changed the subject. "Okay, I need to call Lavinia, too. Where's Strutter? How is she doing today?"

"She's fine. She's handlin' Vista Views again today, if I can get her away from the university's Web cam site, that is. Ever since Jenny showed us that big, disgustin' corpse flower, she's been checkin' it every twenty minutes. Talk to you later." And she was gone.

I remained where I was, phone in my hand, and struggled to put the pieces of this puzzle together. Somewhere, there had to be a connection between two, if not all three, of our tormentors, but I didn't have enough information to figure it out. I had promised to telephone Lavinia, however, so perhaps I could accomplish two things with one call. I retrieved the Henstocks' number from my phone's memory and punched Redial. Lavinia must have been waiting near her phone, because she answered immediately. After assuring her that I had sustained no permanent damage in the previous evening's mishap, and still flushed with virtue from my morning confessional, I gave her the advice she had requested.

"I really think you should tell Ada what you told me last night, Lavinia. She already knows that the Judge probably had a lady friend or two after your mother's death. Besides, secrets always fester." I had had far too many opportunities to see that for myself over the past few years. "Tell Ada exactly what you told me … that you believe that's what you heard, although you don't know what it meant. She's a strong woman. She can take it, and after what happened last night, you need to have her completely aware and on your side."

I had jumped ahead, and Lavinia was understandably perplexed. "Do you mean that there's some connection between what I overheard sixty years ago in Papa's study and our getting locked in the basement? How could that possibly be?"

"As bizarre as it seems, yes, I think there may be a connection." I told her Margo's theory. "We think it's very possible that an intruder was in the house while you and I were in the parlor, looking for what he didn't find on his first visit. That is, your plumber may not have been a plumber at all but someone who knew that your father's private papers were hidden somewhere in the house and was looking for them. Did you ever discover what was stored in that closet, by the way?"

I could almost hear poor Lavinia struggling to make sense of all that I had said. "I'm afraid not, my dear. As we told you, poor Clara, our cook, passed away long since, and our faithful housekeeper Agnes went to her reward two years ago, according to her niece, with whom I spoke a few days ago."

I changed tacks. "I know you found the plumber's ad in a local newspaper, and he gave you a business card that turned out to be bogus, so those leads have been dead ends. Can you describe what he looked like?" I was eager to see if there were physical similarities between the plumber and the Van Man, as I had begun to think of my stalker. I had only seen him the once, standing on my front porch with his back to me. He had been wearing a dark blue or black windbreaker, jeans, and running shoes, which hardly constituted a memorable outfit. About the only distinguishing characteristic I could recall was his closely shaven head.

"Well, let's see. He was young-ish, but not a child. Middle-aged, I guess you'd say, or maybe older."

"What was he wearing?"

She considered the question. "Some sort of dark jacket and denim pants. And a big tool belt, I remember that."

So far, so good. "And what about his hair? What color was it?" I held my breath and waited.

"Why I don't know," she said finally. "He was wearing a knitted cap on his head. I remember wondering about that, because it was such a beautiful morning, much too warm to need a hat."

My heart sank as once again, the puzzle pieces refused to fit together.

12

The next morning, I felt well enough to struggle in to the office—or perhaps the prospect of another day cooped up with only CNN and two somnolent cats for company was the stronger motivator. In the shower, I carefully palpated the bump on my head and didn't see stars. When I found I was also able to manipulate shampoo bottle and hair dryer without too great a protest from my elbow, I covered my discolored toes with a clean sock, strapped the air cast back on, and bid Armando farewell.

Even though it was my left ankle that had been injured, and my Altima had an automatic transmission, the cast made getting into and out of the car a clumsy undertaking, as loaded down as I was with my tote bag and laptop. The paramedics had left a pair of crutches with me, but I knew from experience that they would be more trouble than help, so I left them behind. The swelling was already down considerably, and I promised Armando I would spend as much time as possible with my ankle propped up.

By the time I made it into the Law Barn lobby, half walking and half hopping, I was predictably pretty winded. Jenny rushed to unburden me and helped me navigate the six stairs leading down to the MACK Realty office, where I flopped onto the sofa. To my surprise, Strutter already occupied the desk chair, from which she was staring, heavy-

waved to acknowledge my arrival before returning her attention to the screen.

"Whew! Thanks so much, Jen. I was running out of steam." I grinned at her reassuringly as she fussed around piling up pillows from the sofa to prop my foot, bringing me coffee, and generally acting on her mother hen instincts. Having settled me to her satisfaction, she disappeared back up the stairs to the lobby. Suddenly, Strutter groaned and dropped her head into her hands. I leaned forward in alarm, spilling hot coffee on my hand. "Ouch! Strutter, what's wrong? Are you okay? Is it the baby?"

Strutter raised her head, and her expression did nothing to reassure me. Well, pregnancy at her age was no picnic, especially with a full-time job, an active twelve-year-old at home, and a new husband. "The baby's fine. I'm fine, too, at least so far. Ask me again at the end of the day, and my answer may be very different." She took pity on my obvious confusion and pointed at the computer screen. Once again, it showed the botanical lab at the University of Connecticut in which the much ballyhooed corpse flower was about to blossom into full hideousness. From the number of people standing in line, it was clear that the thing continued to attract hordes of visitors.

I hobbled over to take a closer look. All I saw was the same huge, ugly specimen, although this morning, the turgid bud seemed to have begun to blossom. I scanned the screen and saw the same, fascinated stink groupies moving slowly by in ones and twos. The Web cam clock continued to monitor the time in the top right corner of the screen. "What's the problem? I don't see it."

"Him," she amended tersely. "You don't see him, and neither do I. That's the problem." Wearily, Strutter rose and pushed me into the chair. "Sit down, fool. You're the one who should be off her feet." She took my spot on the sofa. "That guard who's always standing there on the left, moving people along. He's not there today."

"Okay, he's not there. So what? Why do you care about some university employee?"

"I know this one."

"Really? Is he another one of your nephews?" Hartford County was studded with what seemed to be an inexhaustible supply of Strutter's Jamaican relatives. Most were the sons and daughters of her equally stunning sisters, who had migrated to the States from the island around the same time she had.

"I wish," was her sorrowful comment now. "Can you stand to hear about one more drama? If it's any consolation," she grinned briefly, "this one's a beauty."

"Hey, what are friends for?"I assured her, but privately, I was filled with misgivings. I was up to here in unsolved mysteries, and it was still only June. At this rate, it promised to be a summer to remember, but I wasn't at all certain I'd want to.

Strutter smiled her thanks and sighed. "That man's name is Reginald Dubois. I used to be married to him."

With difficulty, I kept my mouth from falling open. Tuttle had been Strutter's name when I met her. She had married John Putnam about a year ago, but I had been vaguely aware of a short-lived, previous marriage that had produced her son Charlie. "Charlie's father?" I finally managed to say.

"Technically speaking, although Reggie was never a father in any real sense."

It's funny how you take your friends on faith. I had always known about Strutter's son, but I had never given a thought to who Charlie's father might be. Strutter had been single when I met her two years before at the law firm where she and I and Margo had all worked. She was such a strong, loving mother, and there were always so many nieces and nephews and cousins around, that her family had seemed complete as it was. Then John had come along.

"Tell me," I said now.

"I'll give you the short version," she promised. "When I first came to the States, I lived in San Diego. I worked as a waitress until I qualified for free tuition at the state university as a California resident. San Diego is a big Navy town, and Reggie was stationed there. We had a whirlwind romance, but I was raised very strictly. The only way he could get me into bed was to marry me." Her mouth twisted wryly. "He got leave and whisked me down to Tijuana, where he filled me with cheap wine and took me to some storefront specializing in hurry-up weddings for sailors in a hurry to bed their girlfriends. I was so naïve, and so drunk, that I went for it."

"Big mistake, huh?" I sympathized.

"Oh, yeah. Charlie was born nine months later to the day. Reggie and I lived in married housing for the enlisted personnel, and I worked as long as I could see past my belly. But as soon as Charlie was born, Reggie got ugly. He started slapping me around pretty regularly, but the first time he shook the baby ..." Her face contorted at the memory. "I left him immediately, of course. I waited for him to report for work, then packed up and moved in with a girlfriend from the restaurant. We took turns taking care of each other's kids when we weren't working."

"Did you report Reggie to the authorities?" I burned with anger on Strutter's behalf.

"No, I didn't want him to know where I was living; but I did approach the Mexican authorities to get a divorce. Here's the dramatic part."

"*Here's* the dramatic part?" I was almost afraid to listen to any more.

"Turns out that place in Tijuana was a sham operation that churned out phony marriage certificates for stupid Americans. Even the ceremony was malarkey, but we spoke so little Spanish, we thought it was the real thing. The only real things about the whole experience were the pesos that changed hands before the ceremony and the baby that arrived nine months later. Otherwise, it was all pure fiction."

I could feel my eyes as big as saucers as I stared at my friend. "So then what did you do?"

"Since I wasn't legally connected to Charlie's father, and I wasn't about to go after him for child support anyway, I decided to cut my losses and just disappear. I packed up the baby and headed for Connecticut to live with Estella and her husband." Estella was one of Strutter's two older sisters, who had a son some ten years older than Charlie. "It took me five years, but I put myself through a legal assistant program at Manchester Community College, went to work at BGB, and got a little apartment for me and Charlie." She shrugged. "End of story."

BGB was the Hartford law firm at which we had worked side by side before joining forces with Margo to start

MACK Realty. "Until you met Margo and me and John came along," I pointed out, eager to get to the happy ending. I was rewarded with a fond glance.

"Until then," she agreed warmly. Her gaze returned to the computer screen. "And now this."

"It's an incredible coincidence that he should turn up in Connecticut, I agree, but Dubois is ancient history. He doesn't know you're here ... or does he?"

Strutter closed her eyes and rubbed her temples slowly. "I didn't think so, but as you say, it's an incredible coincidence that he's here." She opened her eyes. "What other reason would he have to come all the way across the country? I'm afraid he's looking for his son."

"But how would he find Charlie—or you, for that matter?"

"I heard from my girlfriend once or twice after I came east. She said Reggie had been discharged from the Navy but wound up in prison on an armed assault charge very soon after that. Big surprise, huh?" She rolled her eyes. "Obviously, he was released, probably quite a few years ago. And if he knows anything about computers, it wouldn't be hard to trace me, especially with my name all over transaction documents during the past couple of years."

I had to admit the truth of what she said. "But what makes you think he's trying to find you and Charlie? What could he want?"

"His wife and child, that's what." She jumped up from the sofa and paced restlessly to the window. She stared out at Rhett's pen for a moment, then whirled around to face me. "The thing is, I know our marriage was never legal, but I'm not sure Reggie knows it. He may very well think we're still married." She turned to stare out the window again. "It's these poison pen letters, Kate. They're totally connected to that awful corpse flower at UConn, which is where Reggie apparently works now. And despite his violent tendencies, he always thought of himself as an upstanding Christian. There's something about the judgmental, punitive tone of the letters we've been getting."

She made a face at me over her shoulder. "I was raised on fire and brimstone sermons, too, but some of those Old Testament boys are a little over the top for me. I mean, the Bible says you have to stone your mother if she makes clothes out of two different threads. If Reggie knows about me and John and thinks I'm committing adultery, who knows what he's capable of doing?"

I sipped my cooling coffee and gave it some thought. Strutter hadn't been kidding about the drama, and as far-fetched as her story might seem to an outsider, I knew Charlene Tuttle Putnam as well as I knew anyone. If she had connected these seemingly haphazard dots, they could well be part of a dangerous picture. Besides, this was the best lead yet on our poison pen-pal.

"You're right. There are too many coincidences and half-connections here to ignore. That stink-flower is supposed to be in full bloom today or tomorrow, according to the newspapers, and a violent man who may think you're still his wife, even though you never really were, may have it in his mind to punish you for your nonexistent sins. We have to tell John Harkness, and the sooner the better."

Margo chose this moment to sail through the law barn lobby and down the steps to our office, Rhett Butler adoringly at heel. "Have to tell John Harkness what, exactly?" she smiled, looking from one to the other of us. "And how is your poor ankle, Darlin'?"

"I'll survive," I said tersely. "The question at hand is, will Strutter?"

Without missing a beat, Margo flowed elegantly into Strutter's recently vacated seat and folded her hands in her lap.Rhett flopped at her feet and panted happily, overwhelmed at being surrounded by his three biggest fans. "I believe I've missed somethin' here. Now you just tell your Auntie Margo all about it."

* * *

Twenty minutes later, Margo and Strutter were on their way to the Wethersfield Police Department to share this latest development with John Harkness and his team. To his utter delight, Rhett was permitted to accompany them. As Margo put it, "Nothin' is quite so off-puttin' to a would-be attacker as a great, big ol' hound dog." I doubted that affectionate, docile Rhett would deter any assailant older than a toddler, but it didn't hurt anything to let her keep her illusion. On their way through the lobby, they warned Jenny to be on the lookout for a strange man hanging around, particularly if he asked for Strutter, and to give out absolutely no information about their whereabouts. Jenny went on point like a good setter, and I was confident that we were in good hands.

The morning wore on. Every half hour or so, I got out of my chair and hobbled a few steps just to stretch my cramped muscles. I was pleased to note that my ice-packs-alternated-with-heat-packs regimen of the previous day had brought the swelling down considerably on my ankle, and getting around was becoming more manageable. At about eleven o'clock, Margo called to say that she and Strutter were on their way to Vista Views. Under the circumstances, she didn't want Strutter there on her own, and I agreed.

John had sent an investigator up to the University to make inquiries about the guard we presumed was Reggie Dubois. For good measure, he was having a patrol car keep an eye on the Law Barn at regular intervals throughout the day, which I was surprisingly glad to hear. Whatever Dubois's intentions were, I felt certain that he meant Strutter—and perhaps all of us—harm, and I was grateful for any protection we could get.

By noon, Jenny and I were both hungry. She left me to man the phones while she ran up the street to the diner, locking me for good measure. Within minutes, she was back with two huge, chicken salad sandwiches and side orders of the diner's delicious cole slaw. "Any suspicious-looking characters lurking about?" I asked between greedy bites.

"Nope, no one." Her tongue snaked out of the side of her mouth to lick off some dressing. "Not even Fat Squirrel is around, since Rhett isn't here to harass." She sighed with satisfaction and patted her flat stomach. "If I keep this up, I'm going to gain more weight than Strutter by the time her baby arrives. When is she due, by the way?"

I told her that it might very well be a Christmas baby, and she broke into a big grin. "What a Christmas present, huh?" I agreed that it didn't get much better than that. She scooped up our trash and returned to her post, leaving me to my thoughts.

13

By five o'clock, I had completely cleaned up the paperwork that had accumulated during my absence and returned all of the pending phone calls. Despite being propped up for most of the day, my ankle had begun to throb again. I was more than ready to call it a day, so I decided to shut things down and visit the water cooler on my way out in order to swallow another pair of Advils. Predictably, I had hoisted myself out of my chair and taken a couple of painful steps when the phone rang. Annoyed, I hobbled back and snatched the phone from its cradle. "Kate Lawrence," I snapped.

"Oh, dear. I do hope I haven't called at a bad time," quavered Lavinia Henstock, and I immediately felt bad. I flopped back into my chair.

"No, no, not at all," I assured her, lightening my tone. "I'm just used to being able to move around more quickly than this ankle is allowing." *Ooops. That sounded as if I blamed her for the accident.* I changed course hastily. "What can I do for you, Lavinia?"

There was a brief pause. "Is it all right for me to be, uh, candid on this telephone line?"

I was startled. "No one but Jenny, our receptionist, can access this line, and she's gone for the day, if that's what you're concerned about."

"Oh, good. I do feel it's best to be as discreet as possible," Lavinia said, relieved. Despite my assurances, she lowered her voice, presumably to avoid being overheard at her end. "I found it. That is, I believe I found it ... what that plumber must have been looking for all this time."

My heartbeat quickened. "What did you find?"

"It's a box of Papa's old papers," she almost whispered. "Well, more like a bag, an old leather pouch of some sort. It was locked in the bottom drawer of Papa's desk, and it's just stuffed with documents of all sorts. Some are trial records, I think."

I was simultaneously elated and stunned. "It was in the bottom drawer of his desk all this time? In forty years, you and Ada never opened it?"

Lavinia seemed shocked by my suggestion. "Why, no! Papa's desk was strictly off limits to us as children. When he died, his solicitor had his will and bank account numbers and the deed to the house, just everything we needed. Frankly, until now, we had no reason to look any further. In fact, we had forgotten all about that locked drawer."

As flummoxed as I was by the idea of the Judge's desk remaining untouched for four decades, I could almost understand his daughters not wanting to invade their father's privacy, even after his death. The Judge had been a formidable personality. I struggled to keep my tone even.

"After all this time, you still have a key?"

"Oh, no. I don't believe we ever had that."

I stifled the urge to start tearing at my hair. "Then how did you get the drawer open?"

Lavinia giggled conspiratorially. "We used a crowbar, Dear. It was one of the tools that dreadful plumber person left behind, so it seemed fitting. I know it was terrible of us to deface Papa's desk that way, but we were so distraught about you being injured the other night, we were quite determined to put an end to this terrible situation. So when Ada remembered about the locked drawer, we just pried the damned thing open."

I don't know what astonished me more, hearing Lavinia curse or picturing the sisters having at their father's sacrosanct desk with a crowbar. Clearly, there was more to these old ladies than met the eye. I decided to think more about that later. Right now, I was dying to know what they had discovered.

"What did the trial records reveal? Did you find any documentation that might relate to the skeleton in your father's basement closet?"

"I believe we may have, but these papers are all so confusing. I do hate to impose on you yet again, particularly after what happened last time, but Ada and I were hoping that you might ..."

I was already on my feet and shutting down my computer. "I'll be there in twenty minutes," I promised. "I think the best thing to do is to turn those documents over to the police and let them sift through them for leads, so just pack them all up again and wait for me. And whatever you do, keep all the doors locked until I get there."

After gulping down two painkillers, I grabbed my tote bag and hurried to the back door. As the last person out of the building, I punched in the code on the wall panel that would activate the security alarm, then fumbled to shut the big door and turn my key in the outside lock. The system gave you only thirty seconds to accomplish this. If you were not successful, as I knew from sad experience, automated klaxons went off and the outdoor lights flashed embarrassingly until you could get back inside and enter the deactivation code. I found the whole thing a huge nuisance and heaved a breath of relief when I heard the deadbolt slide into place.

Rhett's pen was empty in the lingering dusk, and even the pesky squirrels seemed to have called it a day as I trudged to the gate that opened into the alley behind the Law Barn. Staff habitually parked there, leaving the spaces out front for the clients. At this hour, the only vehicles in the alley were my sedan and what seemed to be the blue painters' van I had seen earlier in the day, which was parked right beside me. The Best Painters sign confirmed my guess, and I envied whoever it was in the neighborhood who was getting their kitchen or bedroom freshened up.

A toolbox sat on the ground between our vehicles, along with a couple of well-used buckets and a pile of plastic drop cloths. Several lengths of pipe leaned up against the van. *Looks like someone else is putting in a long day, too,* I thought, lowering my overloaded tote bag to the ground and fumbling in it for my car's remote door opener. *How much easier life would be if we didn't have to keep track of all these keys and lock everything up all the time.*

It was my last thought before a muscular arm went around my throat from the back, and something hard jabbed me in the back. "Open the car door, and keep your mouth shut," hissed a male voice close to my ear. "One peep and yours will be the next body those nosey friends of yours will find. It won't be pretty, either. A forty-four makes a big hole." His laugh was humorless, and he punctuated his demand with more jabs.

He's lefthanded, I registered calmly, *because he's using it to hold the gun, and his right arm is around my throat. I must make him let go of me, or I won't be able to do anything at all before he shoots me.*

Strangely, I felt no fear, just an odd detachment and abject weariness. My ankle hurt, and my elbow was beginning to throb again. I was fed up with this situation and the people who had created it. I was tired of pompous philanderers and crazed ex-husbands and religious fanatics. I was sick to death of trying to clean up other people's messes. I had already had my life threatened twice in the last two years trying to do so, and the fact that yet another lunatic seemed to be holding me at gunpoint pushed me over the edge. A cold rage settled over me, and my mind cleared wonderfully. I knew quite clearly what I was going to do.

"Hurry up!" he hissed again. I slapped sharply at the arm around my throat and pointed toward my tote bag where it lay at my feet.

"Key's in there," I gasped, exaggerating my distress. "Can't reach it like this."

As I had hoped, he let go of my throat. Instead, he grabbed my right arm above the elbow and squeezed it for emphasis. "Get it! Make it quick!" Pain shot through that abused joint, and I saw stars. I grew even more furious.

I bent over the tote bag and made a show of pushing the contents around, ostensibly to find the opener. A glance to my left confirmed that he was indeed holding a weapon of some sort in his left hand. With my head bent over the tote bag, I raised my eyes enough to spot the lengths of pipe I had noticed leaning against the van. The split second it took me to calculate that they were within my reach was all it took me to decide to go for it. I fumbled in the bag for another moment as I focused on the nearest pipe and mentally rehearsed my move. Before I could lose my nerve, I grabbed the pipe and whirled to bring it crashing down on his gun hand with the full force of my pent-up rage.

My attacker howled in anguish. The weapon fell from his hand and skittered off beneath the van. He fell to his knees, clutching his left arm with his right. I grabbed my tote bag and ran around to the other side of the car, where I managed to let myself in and squirm over the gear shift into the driver's seat. A few seconds more, and I tore recklessly out of the alley. I felt ten feet tall and bulletproof, so full of adrenalin I couldn't have let up on the gas pedal if I had wanted to, which I didn't.

I took Old Main Street at breakneck speed and didn't stop until I reached the well-populated parking lot of the bank on the corner of the Silas Deane Highway. With the car doors locked, I retrieved my cell phone from my pocket and punched 911. When the police dispatcher answered, I gave her a brief summary of what had happened and a description of the van. I asked that Lieutenant Harkness be notified and announced that I would be pulling into the Police Department parking lot in less than five minutes. Then I drove circumspectly out of the lot and down the highway, careful to observe the posted speed limit.

It wasn't until I had parked carefully within the lines of a visitor space in the Police Department lot that the reality of my near miss set in. Had I been out of my mind?

Temporarily, most certainly, but what had my options been? To submit meekly to whatever the brute's demands were with no assurance that he would then let me go? No, the role of victim wasn't my style. Given any sort of choice, I would put up a fight every time, but frankly, I didn't know how many more fights I had in me.

As I turned off the engine, my teeth began to chatter. I began to shake, then whimper. Not long afterward, for the second time in as many years, a nice, young officer found me sobbing hysterically in a police department parking lot and escorted me into the building.

* * *

Shortly before six, a war council of sorts had assembled at the big table in the Henstocks' kitchen. To my left sat John Harkness, who had called this meeting and followed me to Broad Street in his unmarked sedan from the police station. Henry the dog sniffed madly at John's shoes and cuffs, excited by this masculine presence in his kitchen. Occasionally, he yipped sharply in an attempt to get this new alpha male's attention. John ignored him.

I had given my statement to young Sergeant Fletcher, who, unfortunately, was becoming quite accustomed to dealing with incidents involving me and my partners. Beyond expressing appropriate concern for the mother of one of his former schoolmates, he had barely raised an eyebrow to find me once again sitting beside his desk, just gotten right down to business. I was grateful for his matter-of-factness. It helped me get a grip, which John had already indicated I was going to need. The fact that my tormentor had gone to the trouble and expense of painting his van blue, changing the magnetic signs on its doors to "Best Painters," and lurking in the vicinity of the Law Barn for the past several days before actually accosting me indicated premeditation and patience of frightening dimensions. My stalker was real, and he was serious.

"I can't believe I walked right into his set-up. I even saw the pipes leaning against the van, and it never occurred to me to wonder what a painter would need with piping," I groused to Margo, who sat next to me and carefully wrapped another ice pack around my injured elbow, tsk-ing with concern. Across from us was Strutter, hunched bleak-eyed and weary over a cup of tea. Ada and Lavinia alternately perched on either side of her or fluttered about, refilling cups and replenishing our plates with homemade pecan shortbread.

The document-filled leather pouch Lavinia had mentioned sat on the floor next to John, but we had other territory to cover first. "From the outset of this investigation, we have theorized that the individual who has been attempting to intimidate someone at MACK Realty with anonymous poison pen letters might be the same man who posed as a plumber to gain access to this house." John had his small notebook open on the table in front of him. He had self-consciously taken a pair of reading glasses, obviously new, from the pocket of his blazer. They perched on the end of his nose as he referred to his notebook, frowning with concentration. "As of today, we have abandoned that theory."

"But why?" Strutter exclaimed. I groaned in frustration. If only I knew.

Margo patted me absently, her eyes locked on John's face. "Hush, now. We need to pay attention to what John is sayin'." I raised my eyebrows but stayed quiet.

"Because thanks to Mrs. Putnam's lead," John nodded to Strutter in acknowledgment, "we determined this afternoon that your poison pen pal was, in fact, one Reginald Dubois, a University of Connecticut employee assigned to guard duty in the botanical lab."

It was Strutter's turn to groan. "I knew it! As soon as I figured out that was Reggie I was looking at on that Web cam ... but he wasn't there today. Did you find him? How do you know he wasn't the one who attacked poor Kate outside the Law Barn?"

"Arf-arf-arf-arf-arf!" yapped Henry, dancing around John's feet. For the first time, John looked at the little dog directly. He leaned forward slightly.

"No! Now sit," he said firmly. Henry's little butt hit the floor. Margo smiled to herself as the rest of us exchanged astonished looks, and John continued.

"As you know, we dispatched a team of detectives to UConn earlier today to determine Dubois' whereabouts and take him in for questioning, if that seemed warranted. When they arrived at the lab where the so-called corpse flower is housed, they were informed that Dubois had called in sick, citing the overwhelming, uh, odor of the plant as the cause of his headache and nausea. They obtained his home address, which turned out to be a small apartment near campus, and knocked on his door.

Even from across the table, I could tell that Strutter was holding her breath. "Then what, Darlin'?" Margo murmured encouragingly. John shot her a *don't-call-me-*

that-in-public look, and she lowered her eyes with unaccustomed meekness.

"Dubois came to the door and let my detectives in without a problem. His alleged sickness seemed to be genuine, as he was lying on his couch with aspirin and antacid on the table next to him. When questioned about his former relationship with Ms. Putnam and the threatening letters being mailed to her workplace from Storrs, he confessed readily. Whatever the legal situation regarding their marriage, he said, he considered them married in the eyes of God. Therefore, she was an adulteress, and Dubois felt it was his duty to warn her, however oddly, of the repercussions of her behavior." He looked up from his notes and peered at Strutter over the top of his new eyeglasses. "By that, we assume he meant her recent remarriage."

John paused to allow the rest of us to digest his narrative. He looked down at Henry, who remained sitting and quiet at his feet. Casually, he patted the furry head. "Good dog," he said. Henry squirmed with delight and belly-flopped onto the floor.

Ada and Lavinia looked at each other, then back at John. "That's all there was to it?" Ada ventured. "Surely, there must have been more motivation than that to prompt a barrage of hateful letters such as that." Margo and I nodded in agreement.

"Dubois was actually quite docile, according to my investigators. Poison pens often are, when they're confronted. When my men reminded him that Charlene had every right to marry, since his marriage to her in Mexico had not been legal even by Mexican law, and that sending letters of that sort through the U.S. Mail constituted a felony, he backed right down. Apologized, even. My detectives gave him a severe warning and left him lying on his couch."

Mixed with the relief on Strutter's face was cold fury. She stared at John stonily. "And did he once ask after his son? Did he even remember Charlie's name?"

John's eyes and tone, when he answered her, were gentle. "According to the investigators' report, the subject of your son was not raised. I'm sorry. But at least we now know where Dubois is and can keep an eye on him. It's very unlikely that you will be bothered by him again."

Strutter hid her face in her teacup, and I hastened to fill the sudden silence by getting back to the subject of our meeting. "And at least we know that Dubois isn't Van Man, since he couldn't have been talking to John's detectives in Storrs and been assaulting me in Wethersfield at the same time."

John took off the new specs and pocketed them. "You might say that's the good news. The bad news is, the guy in the van is still out there somewhere, and we don't have a good description of him." He threw me an apologetic glance, but it was true. I hadn't gotten the license plate number, and I still couldn't identify my assailant in a line-up. Except for when I turned to smash his left wrist with the pipe, he had been behind me, and after that, I had been intent only on getting into my car and fleeing the scene.

I bristled with what little energy I could summon. "But I know I did some serious damage to his left arm. It might even be broken. The pain would be awful. He would almost have to seek medical help, and that means someone, somewhere must have seen him. He might be sitting in an emergency room right now, for all we know."

There was a general murmur of agreement, and John continued. "From your statement of how he reacted to your ..."

"Self-defense," I inserted coldly.

"Yes, of course, Sugar," Margo soothed, and John grinned at me.

"Yeah, you defended yourself pretty good there," he agreed, and my ire subsided as quickly as it had risen. "I think any of my officers would think twice before taking you by surprise. We have every major medical facility and walk-in center in the region on alert for a left-wrist injury, but there's been no feedback yet. My guess is that no matter how much pain he's in, our guy hasn't gotten what he's after yet, and he's not going to stop until he gets it."

Lavinia, circling the table to refill cups, stopped in her tracks. "But what *is* he after, Lieutenant? Do we even know for certain?"

John met her imploring gaze directly. "Again, all we've got at this point is a working theory, but we think it's a pretty good one, and we have all of you to thank for helping us put it together."

Ada spoke up. "Do stop fussing, Lavinia, and come and sit down. We all need to hear this." Lavinia did as she asked.

"As of this afternoon, we have been able to separate the perpetrator of the poison pen letters from the circumstances surrounding the discovery of female remains, *circa* nineteen-forty-five, in the basement of this house. What we know so far about that is that at some point during or following the construction of a brick-and-mortar compartment next to the boiler, the body of a young-ish white woman was concealed there. On June twentieth of this year, Miss Ada and Miss Lavinia were visited by a middle-aged man purporting to be a plumber, who had been hired to repair a leak in the pipe running between the boiler and the brick enclosure. During the process of partially dismantling the enclosure to gain access to the pipe, he discovered the skeletal remains. From the way he fled the premises, that was not what he had been expecting to find."

John flipped back a few pages and squinted at his notebook. No one suggested that he put on his glasses. "From that point on, it's pure conjecture, but this is what we believe may have happened. While the Henstocks were occupied in the front parlor with Ms. Putnam, the plumber returned through the side door, slipped back into the basement, and removed the remains, probably in a sack of some kind.

"He left the same way and transported the remains, probably in his van, to the Spring Street Pond. How he ever managed to do it in broad daylight beats hell out of me, but somehow he dumped the body into the pond without being noticed and made his escape. Since there wasn't any meat left on the bones ... sorry, Ma'am," he apologized after catching Lavinia's audible gulp, "he probably assumed the skeleton would just sink into the muddy bottom. But there must have been an air pocket in the remaining fabric of the clothes, or it got stuck in the reeds, because Kate's camera caught an image of it when she stopped to take a photo of the swans. We retrieved the body the next morning, and subsequent testing established the approximate age of the victim and time of her death."

He looked up from his notes. "A few nights ago, we believe the same intruder entered the house again from the side door, either before or during Kate's visit with Miss Lavinia, to search for something related to that victim. He made friends with the dog by giving him a treat of some sort, which later allowed him to exit the house without causing a ruckus. Apparently, he still didn't find what he was looking for, because he assaulted Kate this afternoon."

Suddenly, fatigue overcame me, and I was eager to be done with this rehash. A quick glance around the table confirmed that we all shared that feeling. "So now what?" I asked dully.

John lifted the leather pouch from the floor to the table. "Now, I think we may have our first real clue somewhere in these documents." He looked at the sisters, a slow smile spreading across his face. "I understand that you ladies found this in a locked drawer of your father's desk in the study after, uh, forcing it open."

"Why, yes," Ada responded promptly. Papa left everything in this house to Lavinia and me, so we had every right to examine the contents of his desk. When I remembered that the desk had been locked all these years, we tried to think where the key might have got to, but it was no use. So we forced the lock."

"With a crowbar," Lavinia added, for good measure. John beamed at her and shook his head in amazement. His approval of their pro-active approach was apparent.

Lavinia blushed to the roots of her white hair, and even Ada grew a bit rosy.

"Well, let's hope your initiative puts us on the right track to resolve this situation. I'll bring these documents back to the station and put the night-shift detectives right on it. Perhaps they'll have some information for us in the morning." He pushed back his chair, and Henry leaped to his feet, panting adoringly. It was clear that John had made more than one conquest tonight. "In the meantime, everybody remember that Kate's assailant is still out there somewhere, and he's something of a chameleon. Stay alert, and keep everything locked up tight. If anything at all worries you, dial 911 immediately."

He rose to see us all safely to our respective vehicles and gave Henry an approving pat. "How did you get that dog to mind, John?" I couldn't help but ask as Strutter helped the sisters clear the table. Margo had excused herself and gone in search of the powder room.

John looked surprised. "Henry's not a bad little guy. Dogs need to know what's expected of them. Obviously, he was trained by someone before he wound up at the shelter. He just needs to be reminded of his manners, don't you, Fella?" He tugged the dog's ear gently, and Henry wriggled with joy.

"And I know just the one for the job," Margo said, joining us at the door. She and John exchanged knowing looks, and I felt sure that a play date with Rhett Butler was in Henry's future. We all said our goodnights, and Strutter followed us slowly out the side door of the old house. The number of cars in the driveway, as well as the lights blazing uncharacteristically throughout the first floor of the house, must have the neighbors thinking the old girls were throwing one heck of a party. If they only knew.

"I'll call you in the mornin', Sugar," Margo whispered, following John down the porch stairs. "I have the beginnings of an idea about what to do with this fabulous house, but right now," she glanced anxiously at our friend, "I think Strutter needs a hug."

14

In keeping with my newfound determination not to withhold information from Armando, I filled him in on the events of the day when he got home from work. From the force of long habit, I consciously minimized the drama. I even attempted to make light of the attack by pumping my fist in the air in triumph after relating how I had turned the tables and thwarted my assailant.

I was disappointed, even dismayed, to see the color drain from Armando's face during my recitation. He put his mug of tea on the coffee table and leaned his head on one hand. A small tic appeared at the corner of his left eye. "So this thug, this *matón*, has been following you all over town for many days now. He disguised his vehicle to fool you, and today, he waited for you to be alone and assaulted you in the parking lot. Is this accurate?"

I had to admit that it sounded pretty bad, when he put it like that, and I said so.

"What other way is there to put it?" he demanded. "This man means you harm for no other reason than he believes you know the location of some evidence of a past crime. Who knows how this would have ended, had you not gone into your Superwoman mode?" The tic under his eye was becoming more pronounced.

"The good news is that we found out who's been sending us hate mail," I said brightly and spewed out the whole story of Strutter's quasi ex-husband. "Now that the police have had a little chat with him, I don't think we'll be bothered any more, which is a good thing, because Strutter has already had more than enough drama for one week, and I honestly don't think she could handle anything more." I became aware that I was babbling and stopped. "Ready for dinner, Honey?"

"Not yet." Armando turned to face me fully, and I noticed how tired he looked. No, more like *sick* and tired. I realized how great a toll the events of the past week had taken on him. Just moving in with me would have been quite enough for him to handle without having to deal with the stress of recent events in my life. It wasn't my fault, exactly, but given the present circumstances, who could blame him if he were reconsidering his decision to share my roof. "What is the plan of the police to find this man in the van and to protect you until they do?"

I struggled to reassure him. "Unfortunately, I still could not give them a good physical description, since he was behind me throughout the, um, assault. He was wearing pretty much the same thing as always … jeans, windbreaker, knitted hat. He changed the color of the van and the signs on the doors, and he could do that again. And since I didn't get a license plate number …" I shrugged. "But an APB has been issued for a blue van with 'Best Painters' signs and a broken taillight, just in case he doesn't have time to do another make-over. And I did some major damage to his left arm, so he may have to seek medical attention. All of the hospitals and walk-in centers have been put on alert. The Wethersfield Police have the Law Barn on regular patrol during office hours."

"They did that yesterday," Armando commented drily. "I do not see that it has helped much so far."

"But now they have more accurate information to go on." It sounded lame even to me, but what more was there to say? I got to my feet and headed for the kitchen, trying not to limp noticeably, although my ankle was killing me after the day's workout. "Some hot food and a glass of wine will do us both good. Back in a jiffy."

* * *

Saturday morning was clear and lovely enough to serve as an advertisement for summer in New England. For the first time this season, Armando and I took mugs of coffee and the newspaper out onto the back deck to savor the soft breeze and the birdsong that surrounded us. Not for the first time, I was aware that the sounds of the summer birds were distinctly different from those of the starlings, mourning doves, cardinals and crows that stayed throughout the winter. From the wetlands behind our house came the songs of robins, flickers, and of course, the mockingbird with his seemingly endless repertoire. All were busy with the business of feeding the insatiable nestlings that clamored from every treetop.

By the time he was well into his second cup of coffee and the world news, Armando seemed far more relaxed than he had the previous evening. The tic under his left eye had vanished, I was pleased to note. Now if only the police could track down my tormentor, perhaps our lives could get back to normal. Predictably, just as I had settled into lazy consideration of the day's schedule, the phone rang. I got up once again to answer it. There might be some good news from the police about the investigation.

"Kate here," I announced, dropping heavily into the overstuffed chair next to the telephone table.

"Margo here," was the bright reply. Too bright for this hour on a Saturday morning, I speculated, but the reason soon became evident. "How are you today, Sugar?" I opened my mouth to tell her, but she rushed on. "Listen, I have the most incredible idea about the Henstocks' house. It hit me yesterday evenin' when I trotted on down the hall to find the powder room while you were all sayin' your goodbyes, remember? Well, all those old doors look alike, and it's not like they had a sign posted, so I turned a wrong doorknob or two before I found the loo."

"Okay," I said warily. "So what did you find? If you tell me another skeleton fell out of another closet, I'm hanging up."

"Oh, this is much more interestin' than some old bag of bones, Honey. If I'm right, and I usually am about this sort of thing, the Henstock ladies are sittin' in the middle of an absolute treasure trove."

My mind spun busily through what I remembered of the house. "It's a grand old house, Margo, but honestly, it needs such a lot of work ..."

"Not the house, silly woman. The *furniture*. If what I saw piled up in those back rooms downstairs is any indication, those little ol' gals have one of the most fabulous collections of antiques I have ever seen."

I remained skeptical. I have never been one to oooh and aaah over the uncomfortable old horrors that seemed to populate the few antique stores I had visited in my lifetime. Still, I knew many people who did. I remembered the tufted settees and leaded lampshades in the Henstocks' front parlor. "Do you really think that musty old stuff is worth anything?"

"Stuff? *Stuff?* Sugar, I personally know two dealers in Atlanta who would cheerfully slap their grandmas for a chance to get their hands on what I saw last night, let alone whatever else is probably in that house.

"Slap their grandmothers? Who would do such an awful thing?"

"It's just an expression, Hon, sorry. I keep forgettin' how literal you Yankees are. The point is, the Henstocks' house may be fallin' down around their ears, but that furniture is an undiscovered gold mine. I know because antique collectin' was just about Mama and Daddy's favorite thing to do in the world. Daddy's idea of a Sunday drive was a tour of the local antique shops, and instead of *Little Red Ridin' Hood*, Mama read to me from *The Bulfinch Anatomy of Antique Furniture.* I believe they're on a first-name basis with every dealer east of the Mississippi. I can identify periods and designers at fifty paces, and my hunch is, these old gals have nothin' whatsoever to worry about."

My initial skepticism was followed by a wave of elation. I realized how fond I had become of Ada and Lavinia and how worried I had been about the financial future. If what Margo said was true, and it never occurred to me to doubt her, they would be all right even if we didn't succeed in selling their house.

"But that's wonderful!" I exulted. "Have you told Ada and Lavinia yet?"

I could hear the smile in Margo's voice. "No, Sugar. After everythin' you've been through on their behalf, I thought you might like to help me do that. Of course, we need to convince them to let us bring one or two dealers through the house to inventory what's there and put a value on it. But wait. I haven't told you the best part."

"There's more? Tell me, tell me." I was suddenly greedy for more good news.

"This part was Strutter's idea. She was feelin' so blue last night about that dreadful Reggie person and his not even givin' a damn about his own son that I followed her home. Her hubby and Charlie went out to pick up pizza, and I told her about my discovery at the Henstocks to distract her from the general awfulness of the day. It worked."

Margo chuckled with satisfaction. "I could see the wheels just turnin' and turnin' behind those gorgeous eyes of hers. Then she said, 'I'll bet the right investor could turn that house into the antiques showcase of New England. You know how the collectors flock to this part of the country. Wethersfield is a huge draw already. Just imagine that house fully restored to its original glory and completely furnished with authentic period pieces. It could be a bed-and-breakfast, just the way you thought. But this one would be especially for antique lovers, and every stick of furniture would be for sale ... for the right price, of course.' How about that for an idea?"

"Wow. It sounds wonderful, but the initial investment would have to be enormous ..."

"Oh, pish, tosh," Margo dismissed my practical concerns. "There you go worryin' about money again.

I've already told you, one call to Atlanta, and I'll have dealers lined up on the ladies' doorstep competin' with each other to submit a proposal. All we have to do is sell the idea to Ada and Lavinia. Do you think they'd be willin' to consider it?"

I considered the question. The Broad Street house had been the sisters' home for more than eighty years. They had never known another. Reluctantly, they had come to grips with the need to sell the actual structure, if they could; but how could they give up all the lovely furnishings inside the house, as well? It seemed almost too much to ask.

"It's an incredible idea, Margo. It could absolutely be the answer, but can Ada and Lavinia accept the idea of losing their house and most of their belongings, too, in exchange for financial security? I just don't know. All we can do is lay out the idea and see what they say. How is Strutter doing, by the way?"

"By the time I left her last night, she seemed more like her old self than I've seen her in a long time. I think it did her good to have somethin' else to think about for a while. I know it picked me right up," Margo confirmed. "What with one thing and another, this has been one of the most depressin' weeks I can remember. It's about time the tide turned."

I agreed. "Maybe the police will find the lead they need among those documents John took away last night, and it will help them get Van Man out of the picture. If they do, and we can all go back to our routine business, I swear I'll never complain about having a boring day again. Have you heard anything from John yet?"

"Not yet, but I'm expectin' him to call any minute now. I'd like to have good news for the ladies about the investigation before we talk to them about our idea. Talk to you later, Hon." And she was gone.

I replaced the phone in its cradle in better spirits than I could recall enjoying in some time. Maybe Margo was right. Perhaps her discovery at the Henstocks' house was a sign that things were beginning to go in our favor. I got up with a smile on my face and went back outside to tell Armando the good news.

* * *

Thanks to my partners' creative thinking and Mother Nature's dazzling display of early summer weather, my mood improved steadily throughout the morning. As is the case for most women who work outside the home, Saturdays were reserved for the domestic tasks and errands that accumulated during the week. At least I didn't have soccer practice and Cub Scout field trips to contend with any more, I comforted myself as I slogged through the third load of laundry and pushed the vacuum cleaner around the downstairs rugs.

Upstairs, Armando wrestled with his electronics, setting up his complicated stereo system and hooking up his computer and printer in the loft that overlooked the living room. Just a few years ago, when I had moved into The Birches, he had served as my volunteer electrician and done the same things for me. It seemed kind of silly for us each to have our own audio and computer systems, not to mention separate phone lines, but that appeared to be the situation when middle-aged people merged households.

After years of having everything exactly the way we wanted it in our individual abodes, it took the edge off our anxieties about living together if we didn't have to share absolutely everything. Presumably, we would adjust to this new state of affairs and be able to operate in a more blended environment in time.

By early afternoon, we were ready to tackle the most pressing of the weekend errands. We set out to do the grocery shopping at the local Stop 'n' Shop and managed to get that done fairly amicably. I had long ago learned to split up the list and take separate carts so he wouldn't be hovering over me and second-guessing my every choice. It wound up being a little bit more expensive, since we might wind up getting both black and Spanish olives, instead of one or the other; but at least we didn't have to stand there debating our preferences in the aisle before one of us deferred to the other.

We loaded up the car and considered lunch options. A sandwich at the diner now, or a trip to visit the swan family at the Spring Street Pond, followed by coffee and Italian cookies at Modern Pastry on Franklin Avenue? We opted for the latter and headed for the pond.

"There they are!" I leaned forward eagerly, camera at the ready, as Armando drove slowly along the sandy road next to the grass verge. The splendid weather had brought easily a dozen visitors to the pond this afternoon, who were busy ignoring the "Do Not Feed the Animals" sign and pitching all sorts of bread, popcorn and other dreadful stuff to the waterfowl. *At the very leas they could put down cracked corn,* I fumed silently, but there was apparently no convincing people that they were doing more harm than good with their offerings. I shook off my irritation and concentrated on capturing the entire swan brood in one photo, but the cygnets wouldn't cooperate. Along with the ducks and a few geese, they kept lunging for the limp bread and other garbage that would gum up their digestive tracts and keep them from foraging for the pond greens and other nutritious natural food available to them.

"They are becoming little beggars, are they not?" Armando, too, looked sad. "I do not like to see them so dependent on, how do you say it, handouts? Especially when this food is not good for them." He opened the door on his side of the car. "Give me the camera, *Cara*. Your ankle needs a rest. Perhaps I will have more luck from outside the car."

Although my ankle wasn't bothering me, I was happy to turn over photography duty to Armando. As he tried to get a better angle, a jogger with a large, golden retriever on a leash ran by the group of spectators. Predictably, the excited dog began to bark, and the water fowl on the bank immediately dispersed.

The large cob went into defense mode, raising his wings and back feathers while lowering his head. An ugly hiss was directed at the retriever, regardless of the fact that he and his master had passed by without incident, while the pen herded their young ones back into the water. The little flotilla was soon foraging peacefully by the far bank, and Armando snapped two pictures for Emma's weekly swan report. "Did you see how the littlest one tips up like a teapot when he feeds underwater instead of just dipping his neck down like the others?" I commented as he got back into the car.

Armando smiled. "I thought you would notice that. Yes, he has to do things a little differently than the rest of them. Perhaps his neck is not yet as long as theirs are, but he will catch up. In the meantime, he will do what he must to survive."

As we watched, the mother swan and three of the cygnets dipped their heads below the surface, where a particularly lush growth must be. The fourth youngster dunked his head, as well, but in order to reach the greens, he went from horizontal to vertical, tail feathers waggling. His parents seemed entirely unconcerned by his unconventional approach to dining, and I couldn't help but laugh. Among water fowl, as among human beings, adaptability and compromise seemed to be important keys to survival, I told myself and grinned at my mate.

"Italian cookies or cannoli for lunch?" I asked, and we were soon on our way to the famous Franklin Avenue bakery, where we enjoyed fresh coffee and delicious pastry. As always, we shared space at the homey, old-fashioned counter with a cross-section of the neighborhood, including a young couple and their infant son, who kept us entertained with his cheerful gurglings. After a pleasant half hour or so of coffee and conversation, we paid our ridiculously reasonable check and made our farewells to the other patrons.

"Do you suppose Emma or Joey will ever make us grandparents?" I wondered aloud as we got back into the car for the trip home.

"Unless we are married, you are the only one who will become an *abuela*," Armando responded, ever the stickler for accuracy. "But should that day ever come, at least I will know where to order the wedding cake."

The ride home passed in companionable silence. Our satellite radio was tuned to the symphony channel, and I was thrilled to be treated to one of my all-time favorite pieces, the "Bach Toccata and Fugue in D Minor." The transcription for large orchestra had its charms, but nothing gave me goose bumps like the original composition for the organ.

We pulled into the driveway, lost in the final, thundering chords. Armando pushed the remote garage door opener and pulled the Altima inside. "Just worry about getting yourself safely up the stairs, and leave the groceries for me to unload. I will go and check the mail." So saying, he let himself out of the car and headed back down the driveway to the mailbox.

Still glowing from the music, I gathered my purse and pushed myself out of the passenger seat, awkward in my aircast. From out of nowhere, Van Man materialized in front of me. I was minimally aware that it must be he from the way he was dressed. He wore the same windbreaker and jeans as he had the day before, although the knitted cap was noticeably missing. He also seemed to be much older than the Henstocks had estimated.

The majority of my brain cells failed to make the switch from contentment to alarm. It seemed so improbable to be confronted by my assailant in my own garage in the middle of such a lovely afternoon. And where was the van? I frowned at him vaguely.

"Please," he said. His face, haggard and unshaven in the daylight, was ashen, and his left arm hung limply at his side. He made no move toward me, but his eyes sought mine. "Please," he said again.

On his way back to the garage to get the groceries, Armando saw the stranger and stopped dead, the mail unheeded in his hand. It took him two seconds to replay the events of the past twenty-four hours in his head, conclude that this must be my attacker, and charge to my rescue. He dropped the mail and tackled Van Man from behind, wrapping both arms around his throat.

Still cushioned by disbelief, I watched the scene unfold. Somehow, I had the presence of mind to fumble for my cell phone in my purse. If one of us was about to get shot, it seemed prudent to call 911; but Van Man made no move to produce a weapon. In fact, he put up no struggle whatsoever and began to totter in Armando's unwilling embrace. Before I could decide whether to call the cops or try to help Armando bring him down, the intruder made the decision for me. His eyes rolled back in his head, and he fell backward in a dead faint, bringing Armando down with him on the garage floor.

"Jesus, Mary and Joseph," commented our neighbor Mary. She stood in the open doorway holding our dropped mail in one bony hand. "It's always something with you two. Who's this guy now?"

"We're not positive, but we think it's the same man who tried to break in here last weekend," I responded automatically. "Do us a favor and call 911, would you, Mary? I need to help Armando." I handed her my phone and crouched down next to him. "Are you all right?"

"Ouch," he said succinctly.

A Skeleton in the Closet

* * *

"Hey, *hombre*, how's it going?" The young Latino EMT who had checked me out earlier in the week greeted Armando on the way into our condo twenty minutes later. Sitting in the overstuffed armchair with an icebag held against the impressive lump that had bloomed on the back of his head, Armando lifted a hand briefly in acknowledgment. As I stood in the front hall surveying the group assembled in my living room, I wondered sourly how many other people in town were on a first-name basis with fully half of the police force and several of the volunteer paramedics. As grateful as I was for their help, it wasn't a distinction I relished.

Once again, our driveway was crowded with emergency vehicles, red lights strobing. I could only imagine the entertainment we were providing the neighbors. Based on Armando's Colombian ethnicity, some of them probably assumed we were running a drug cartel out of our kitchen. A few of the more intrepid spectators were gathered across the street with Mary, who obviously delighted in her role as first-on-the-scene. Well, I sighed inwardly, at least she could set them straight on the drug thing.

I turned away from the front door and backed into the kitchen to make way for the EMTs, who were negotiating the hallway with Van Man strapped onto a gurney. He had recovered consciousness only briefly after Armando had thrashed his way out from under him in the garage. In perhaps the most surreal sequence of the afternoon, we had found ourselves helping the assailant up the stairs into our house, where he sagged into unconsciousness once again on the living room sofa. Whatever his actions had been earlier in the week, he was clearly unarmed and on his last legs this afternoon. Simple humanity required us to offer him minimal assistance until the professionals arrived. Although I had acted purely to defend myself, I couldn't help having a twinge of conscience when I realized how badly the man's arm was hurt and how great a toll the pain had taken on him.

At least it hadn't taken long to give the police my statement this time. After turning over the suspect to them, what was there to say? He had appeared from nowhere, said "please" twice, and passed out, taking Armando down with him. "Please what?" asked the young officer taking careful notes.

"I have no idea," I replied honestly. "That was the extent of his conversation. When he came to, we got him into the house and onto the couch, and he passed out again. He offered no resistance and absolutely no information."

"And he didn't threaten you or Mr. Velasquez?"

"Not me, certainly, and I don't think you can count passing out on top of Armando as a threatening move. Of course, Armando may feel differently about it."

The look Armando threw me might have qualified as life-threatening, but he kept silent. I missed John Harkness and Rick Fletcher, whose senses of humor had humanized former such sessions. This fellow was as buttoned-up as they come. He finished writing and slapped his notebook shut. "Thank you, Ma'am. We'll need you to come down to the station to sign your statement and formalize the charges against this man."

Strangely, considering the events of the past week, a reluctance to file charges overcame me. What had this man actually done to me, besides frighten me half to death? Now that I had seen his face and witnessed him lying unconscious on my sofa, he had become more of a person to me than an assailant. My fear of him had been replaced by curiosity about what had made him behave so menacingly. For the moment, however, I kept my misgivings to myself, not at all sure that this officious youngster would understand them. *John would,* I thought sadly. *Rick would.* And then, affectionately, *Armando will.*

"What will happen to him now?" I asked the officer.

"The perp? He'll receive medical attention at Hartford Hospital and probably go into a secure infirmary. When he's *compos mentis,* he'll be informed of the charges against him, arrested, and have an opportunity to contact an attorney." He got to his feet. "We'll be in touch."

The officer and his partner, who had been across the street taking Mary's statement before the interested crowd, followed the emergency medical van out of the driveway in the gathering dusk. I gave Mary a thumbs up and closed the front door firmly. I had had all the visitors I could stand for one afternoon. I trailed back down the hall to where Armando still sat in the living room. "So?" he said conversationally.

"So what?" I responded forlornly.

"So what is going on in that head of yours? I know it is something. Spit it out." He punched up the icepack and returned it to the back of his head.

I couldn't help smiling at how well he knew me. *"Muy macho, eh hombre?"* I twitted him. "It's not every man who can take having a two-hundred-pound assailant pass out on top of him. You are definitely my hero."

"Fine. You will tell me when you are ready. In the meantime, where is the remote control?" He made himself more comfortable in the chair.

I handed him the remote and his cell phone. "Enjoy yourself, and order a pizza for dinner. I'll bring you a glass of wine in a few minutes. I just need to use the land line to make a phone call first."

He nodded, already busy surfing through the channels. "Margo or Strutter?"

"I'll call them later, but first …"

"Tell Emma I said hello," he said.

15

The following morning, Margo, Strutter and I were lingering in our favorite booth at the Town Line Diner, where Sherri refilled our coffee cups yet again. John Harkness had joined us, but Armando had opted to stay at home, nursing a headache.

Breakfast had long since come and gone. We had a lot to talk about. I had brought my partners up to speed by telephone the previous evening on Saturday's events, but John had news to share about the results of Van Man's interrogation. This time, he didn't need to refer to any notes to remember the details.

"The man who assaulted Kate is named Michael Armentano," he began. The rest of us exchanged puzzled looks. The name meant nothing to us. "No, you wouldn't recognize it. He's a complete stranger to you, as well as to the Henstock sisters. And as you may have already guessed, he's not really a plumber, which explains why we couldn't find him or his company. Throughout this caper, he was operating under an alias."

"Caper? So he did intend to commit a crime," I observed as John sipped his cooling coffee.

"Hard to call it a crime, really, in anything but the strictest technical sense. He didn't even break into the Henstocks' house, if you recall. The door was always open, and Henry was pretty easily dissuaded from his watchdog duties with a handful of raw sirloin. Armentano didn't actually hurt anyone. Kate did far more damage to him than he did to her," he grinned at me.

"That was self-defense," I protested, feeling a bit guilty as I remembered my violent attack on what had turned out to be a senior citizen. "He was holding a gun on me!"

Margo and Strutter nodded in vigorous agreement, but John shook his head. "Sorry, Slugger, but what you thought was a gun turned out to be nothing more than a plastic water pistol that he brandished to get you to cooperate. Guess he didn't know who he was tangling with." He smiled to soften the effect of his words. "Good thing he didn't pull that trick on Margo. She would have ripped off one of her shoes and killed him with a spike heel." Margo and Strutter giggled, and I subsided.

"So what was the crime that this Michael Armentano, not really a plumber, intended to commit but didn't actually?" Strutter brought us back to the business at hand.

"Michael Armentano is the son of one Adrian Armentano, a very elderly man now in his final days at the hospice in Branford," John continued. Back in the nineteen-forties, Adrian was a mason. Judge Henstock hired him to build his document lock-up in the basement in nineteen-forty-five. During the course of the construction work, Adrian asked the Judge to represent his wife, Marianna, in the settlement of a dispute with a local tradesman, which he did a little too assiduously, if you get my drift."

Strutter and I exchanged puzzled looks. "You'd best spell it out, Darlin'," Margo prompted. This time, I noted, John didn't object to the term.

"As you know, Kate, Lavinia Henstock suspected that her father had been inappropriately involved with a local woman. Turns out she was right. The woman was Marianna Armentano, Adrian's wife and Michael's mother. They were having an affair," John stated bluntly.

"Huh! Lavinia's intuition was right on the money," I commented. "So then what happened?"

"Michael Armentano was an infant when all this happened, but way back then, Adrian was a hot-blooded Italian in his mid-twenties. He found out about his wife's affair with the Judge, as Marianna feared he had. That was the conversation Lavinia overheard in the Judge's study that night when she found the door locked. Adrian told Michael a few weeks ago on his deathbed that he had confronted his wife. When she attempted to deny it, he struck her so forcefully that he snapped her neck. She died almost instantly."

We sat, coffee untouched, mesmerized by the tale that was unfolding.

"Adrian was overcome with remorse. He wanted to kill himself, he told Michael, but he had his infant, and now motherless, son to consider. So he did what he felt he had to do at the time. He wrapped his wife's body in a tarpaulin. Then he waited for the Judge to shut himself up in his study the following evening and Ada to go out with her friends. He let himself in the side door of the Henstock house using the key he knew the Judge left under a planter on the porch. He made his way quietly to the basement, carrying his wife's concealed body, and bricked her up behind a false rear wall he created in the closet using leftover materials that were still stacked down there. Then he let himself out the same way. He was betting that if the body was ever found, the authorities would assume it had been the Judge, not he, who had killed her. In a way, it sort of was," John opined.

By this time, I was on the edge of my seat, but John still hadn't answered my most burning questions. "That doesn't explain what Michael Armentano was searching for so desperately that he would break into the house and then pretend to hold a gun on me for information."

John sighed heavily. "You're right. There's more. For over sixty years, Adrian kept his secret, but on his deathbed, he confessed to his son."

"But why?" Strutter vocalized the question on the tip of my tongue.

"Originally, Adrian told Michael that his mother had been having an affair with the Judge, and he had had a terrible fight with Marianna over it. But he told the child Michael that Marianna had returned to the old country in fear for her life, not that he had killed her. In the intervening years, it had occurred to him that the Judge might have kept something, love letters from Marianna or at least papers relating to Henstock's representation of her, that might lead the police to Adrian, if her body were ever found. He didn't want Michael to have to bear that shame. So he made a dying confession to his son and asked him to get back into the Henstock house and look for those documents. He assumed they would be in the basement closet. But when Michael got in, posing as a plumber, there was nothing in the closet. Then something about the back wall of the closet looked wrongto him. He took a hammer to it, and out fell ..."

"Oh my God," I said loudly, imagining the horror. Strutter got the picture at the same time and covered her face, groaning. The patrons at nearby booths looked over curiously. Margo shushed us.

"You've got it," John agreed. From behind the bricks fell the skeleton of dear old Mom. Naturally, Michael freaked, but when he pulled himself together a little while later, he realized that he would be questioned by the police, and DNA testing would link the remains to him, thereby directly implicating his father. So he came back with an empty gunny sack and disposed of Mom in the Spring Street Pond. More bad luck for him, though. The skeleton snagged on the reeds, and along came Kate with her camera."

I sagged back against the back of the booth, my head whirling. "But he couldn't have known about that," I said, still confused.

"Newspaper story," said Margo and Strutter together. "And then there you were, runnin' in and out of the Henstocks' house with the police on a regular basis over the next few days," Margo continued, patting me sympathetically. "In his half-crazy state of mind, he figured you had to have the documents his father had sent him to get, or at least know where in the house the Henstocks had them hidden."

"But Ada and Lavinia didn't even know about them at that time!"

"No, but they knew Michael was looking for something. So they went looking on their own and turned up that leather pouch in dear Papa's desk."

"That reminds me," Strutter jumped in. "What was in that old pouch anyway?"

John smiled his quirky smile at her. "Exactly what everyone thought was in it ... love letters from Marianna Armentano to Judge Henstock and records of his earlier representation of her in court."

"Why would the Judge have kept those things? And why weren't they in that closet? After all, that was why he had it built, wasn't it?" That part still didn't make sense.

John nodded. "Good question. As best we can figure it out, Judge Henstock had to be aware of Marianna's sudden disappearance. He knew Adrian had learned of their affair, because Marianna had told him so. He probably figured out that Adrian Armentano had done something violent and kept those records and letters as a kind of insurance against his being dragged into it. If Marianna turned up dead, and Armentano tried to pin the murder on Henstock, the Judge figured he could produce evidence of a motive for Armentano, jealousy caused by his wife's betrayal."

We all pondered that for a moment. "It's such an incredible sequence of events, but I guess that's what happens when secret builds upon secret," I mused.

"Sooner or later, the skeletons come out of the closet," Margo agreed, "literally, in this case."

Strutter sat with a still-skeptical look on her face. "Assuming everything Michael told you is true, and that's one hell of an assumption, how did he manage to be the one the Henstock sisters called when they needed a plumber? There's about a hundred different ones listed in the Yellow Pages. And how did he even know that they would need a plumber?"

This time, it was Margo who answered the question. "That's where life really gets stranger than fiction. You couldn't make this stuff up. As luck would have it, before Adrian Armentano was diagnosed with terminal lung cancer, he was a regular bingo player. Once a month at the congregational church hall, just like clockwork. Remind you of anyone?"

I thought for a moment. "Ada Henstock! That's where she was the night Lavinia and I got stuck in the basement."

"Right you are, Sugar. And accordin' to John, Ada remembers the old man well. They used to sit by each other sometimes. One night, she mentioned to the people at their table that there seemed to be a leak in the wall behind an old closet her daddy had built in the basement, and could anyone recommend a plumber to take a look-see? I guess Adrian's blood just ran cold. He put two and two together, and very shortly thereafter, Michael appeared at the Henstocks' kitchen door with a phony name and a phony business card to go with it."

John finished the sad story. "Adrian's guilty conscience and fear of discovery prompted a stroke, and that's when they found the cancer."

We were all quiet for a moment. "Poor Michael," I said finally. "Poor little boy, believing he had been abandoned by his mother all those years. And then he found out that the truth was even worse." Strutter reached over and covered my hand with hers.

"I know," she said.

"He didn't really hurt me, and he's suffered enough for the sins of his father, not to mention those of his mother. I'm not going to press charges."

"I know," said John.

"Armando and I are thinking about getting married," I said, apropos of nothing.

Margo snorted into her coffee cup, which never failed to astonish me. "Sugar, we *all* know that."

Epilog

The group assembled in the Henstock sisters' parlor comprised most of the people you would expect on such an occasion. I liked the new way of including men in wedding and baby showers. It had always seemed inappropriate to me to limit attendance at such events to women. Men's roles in marriage and child-rearing are equally critical, after all.

Across the room, Margo and John Harkness, joined by Rhett Butler, were giving Henry the dog the attention he craved. Strutter and her husband visited with Lavinia and Ada on the tufted settee beneath the big front windows. In another corner, Emma had Joey and his steady girlfriend Justine pinned to the wall. She was grilling her brother mercilessly on his intentions. Justine appeared to be listening to his answers with interest, as would I later in the day when Emma relayed them to me. Despite his attentiveness to Emma in Boston, or perhaps because of it, Officer Ron had apparently failed to make the cut in my daughter's eyes. "Too available," she had summed up the relationship, and I knew that Officer Ron was out of luck.

Before proceeding to the Broad Street house on this sunny November afternoon, Armando and I had stopped at the Spring Street Pond, where the young swans were now sleek adults almost ready to strike out on their own. I wondered at the adults' ability to complete the nurturing cycle on a yearly basis. After a summer of intense parenting, did they accept the cygnets' departure each November with aplomb, or did they feel abandoned? Did they anticipate their empty nest with relief or dread? And did former hatchlings ever visit the old folks or even recognize them if they met by accident in the wild? It seemed unlikely.

By next summer, this young foursome would be well and truly launched, caught up in the annual cycle of life with their own mates. Their memories of this summer would be obliterated by the extreme demands of procreation and survival. I reflected that their detachment was enviable, protecting them, as it did, from the heartbreaking goodbyes that punctuate the lives of human beings. Young ones would come and go, and the old ones would live and die, as naturally and inexorably as the changing of the seasons.

In contrast to the protective behavior they had exhibited throughout the summer, the parents foraged serenely today on the opposite side of the pond from their offspring, content in each other's company. The youngsters drifted elsewhere in twos. As if to answer our unspoken concern about the smallest swan's ability to make it on his own, he swam close to us and dipped his head gracefully down, down beneath the water. His aft section remained solidly on the surface as he stretched his neck and pulled busily at some weeds. When he surfaced, he tossed his elegant head as if to say, "See? I've got it!" Armando and I exchanged grins and bumped knuckles, then continued our walk to the party scheduled at the Henstocks' house.

Against all odds, Armando and I had been living together successfully for nearly five months. Oh, it wasn't perfect. We had absolutely gone for each other's throats on a couple of occasions, and not over lofty philosophical issues either. When two strong-willed, independent people share living space, it's not the great questions of life that light the fuse. It's who threw his new red shirt into the washing machine with my white things.

After all of the hullaballoo and news clippings we had endured about the University of Connecticut's corpse flower, the thing never really opened fully. A couple of days after the expected bloom date, reports were issued that while a partial bloom had been accomplished, the corm had never reached full flower. "Nipped in the bud," as Strutter reported to us wryly, "just like Reggie's plans to punish me for what he imagined were my sins." We were all delighted to have that incident behind us, since Strutter's pregnancy was now in full flower.

When we arrived at the Broad Street house, we took a moment to appreciate how grand the old lady was looking. True to her word, Margo had produced a dealer-investor who had rummaged through the house in an ecstasy of discovery with Ada's and Lavinia's enthusiastic approval. Two days later, he had assembled a group of investors and presented the ladies with an offer they didn't even think of refusing. Although much work remained to be done, it was clear that sometime during the next summer, 185 Broad Street would be completely restored and functioning as an elegant bed-and-breakfast establishment. Until the work was finished, the sisters would remain in residence. Then they would withdraw to a snug little Cape Cod house, already purchased and renovated, that adjoined the Broad Street property at the rear. Miraculously, it had come onto the market in September, and Margo moved swiftly to close the deal. The sisters would be comfortably close at hand to serve as docents at their old homestead from time to time and occasionally as hostesses for teas, showers, and other elegant events for which the big house was being readied. They gave every indication of looking forward to their new roles.

We let ourselves into the kitchen through the side door and stood listening to our friends gathered down the hall. "This entryway has seen a lot of grisly comings and goings," I reflected, thinking about the events of the past sixty-plus years.

Armando nodded somberly. "We cannot erase what has happened in the past, *Cara*, but perhaps future traffic through this room will be of a happier kind. We are certainly getting off to a good start today, are we not?"

I smiled up at him. "We are indeed. Let's go celebrate Margo's engagement to John. By the way, speaking of engagements ... is your proposal still open?" I tugged gently at his ear.

He swatted my hand away. "It is open, yes, but you are not ready yet. In truth, neither am I. Ask me again when we have lived together for a year. We will both know better then."

"A year, huh?" I pretended to pout. "How can I be sure you will still be here?"

"I will be here," he assured me. "Now let us see if we can make our way to the front room without having to call the police or the paramedics."

And against all odds, we did.

Meet Judith K. Ivie

A lifelong Connecticut resident, Judith Ivie has worked in public relations, advertising, sales promotion, and the international tradeshow industry. She has also served as administrative assistant to several top executives.

Along the way, Judi also produced three nonfiction books, as well as numerous articles and essays. Her nonfiction focus is on work issues such as two-career marriages, workaholism, and midlife career changes. Second editions of *Calling It Quits: Turning Career Setbacks to Success* and *Working It Out: The Domestic Double Standard* are available from Whiskey Creek Press in trade paperback and downloadable electronic formats.

A couple of years ago, Judi broadened her repertoire to include fiction, and the Kate Lawrence mystery series was launched.

Whatever the genre, she strives to provide lively, entertaining reading that takes her readers away from their work and worries for a few hours, stimulates thought on a variety of contemporary issues-and gives them a laugh along the way.

Please visit www.JudithIvie.com to learn more about all of her books, or use the order form at the back of this book to order her other titles. Judi loves to hear from readers at Ivie4@hotmail.com.

Use this handy order form to enjoy other Kate Lawrence mysteries:

Title	Quantity	Price	Subtotal
Waiting for Armando		@$14.95	
Murder on Old Main Street		@$14.95	
A Skeleton in the Closet		@ $14.95	
		Subtotal:	
		CT residents add 6% tax	
		Shipping & handling @ $2.25 per book	
		Total enclosed:	

Mail with your check and shipping instructions to:

Mainly Murder Press

PO Box 290586 • Wethersfield, CT 06109-0586
www.mainlymurderpress.com

**or save 20% by using PayPal to order online at
www.mainlymurderpress.com**

CPSIA information can be obtained at www.ICGtesting.com
Printed in the USA
BVOW03s1346270414

351807BV00001B/24/P

9 780615 268996